"Written with skill, humanity and a vibrant passion for its subject, the book is irresistible... Physical, spiritual – Arthurian, even – this is true enchantment."
Jan Mark, *TES Teacher*

"This book has something for every reader, not least those who revel in excellent writing."
The Guardian

"The best football novel for children ever... The football is great, the story is fascinating and the ending is spine-tingling. An exceptional experience!"
John McLay, *Carousel*

"You do not need to be a football fan to enjoy the mystery and celebration encompassed in this novel."
The Bookseller

"A remarkable and absorbing story with football at its heart, but superb storytelling in its soul."
Branford Boase Award panel

"This is a tremendous book, profoundly moving, dizzyingly conceived."
School Librarian

"Mal Peet [takes] the football novel into a new league."
The Guardian

By the same author

The Penalty
Tamar

Keeper

MAL PEET

WALKER BOOKS
AND SUBSIDIARIES

LONDON · BOSTON · SYDNEY · AUCKLAND

First published 2003 by Walker Books Ltd
87 Vauxhall Walk, London SE11 5HJ

This edition published 2006

2 4 6 8 10 9 7 5 3 1

Text © 2003 Mal Peet
Cover illustration © 2006 Phil Schramm

This book has been typeset in Horley and Locarno Light

Printed and bound in Great Britain by Creative Print and Design (Wales), Ebbw Vale

British Library Cataloguing in Publication Data:
a catalogue record for this book
is available from the British Library

ISBN-13: 978-1-4063-0393-3
ISBN-10: 1-4063-0393-3

www.walkerbooks.co.uk

*For my children
and other supporters*

PAUL FAUSTINO SLID a blank into the tape recorder and stabbed at a couple of buttons. Then he slapped the machine and said, "Who is the top football writer in South America? Who is the number one football writer in South America?"

The man looking out of the window didn't turn round. There was a smile in his voice when he said, "I don't know, Paul. Who?"

"Me. I am. And will the boss buy me a decent tape recorder? No, she will not." He slapped the machine again and a green light came up on the display. Faustino immediately sat down in front of the small microphone and spoke into it.

"Testing. Date August second. Tape one. Interview: Paul Faustino of *La Nación* talks to the greatest goalkeeper in the history of the world, the man who two days ago took in his hands the World Cup in front of eighty thousand fans and two hundred and twenty million TV viewers."

He jabbed buttons, rewound the tape and played it back.

Faustino's office was on the seventh floor of a block perched on one of the hills that looked down on the city. The big man standing at the window found it easy enough to imagine himself a hawk coasting over the grid of buildings and the drifting white and red lights of the traffic. Somewhere beyond that carpet of lights and just below the edge of the stars was the forest.

He was tall, exactly six feet four inches, and heavy with it. But when he turned from the window and went to the table where Faustino was sitting, his movements were light and quick, and it seemed to the football writer that the big man had somehow glided across the room and into the chair opposite his.

"Are you ready to begin, Gato?" Faustino had his finger on the *pause* button. On the table between them there was a desk lamp that threw hard shadows onto the faces of the two men; also, two bottles of water, a jug filled with ice, Faustino's packet of cigarettes. And a not very tall chunk of gold. It was in the shape of two figures, wearing what looked like nightdresses, supporting a globe. It was not very beautiful. From where Faustino was sitting, it looked rather like an alien with an oversized bald head. And every footballer in the world wanted it.

The World Cup. It burned in the lamplight.

The big man folded his huge hands together on the tabletop. "So. Where shall we begin?" he said.

"With some background stuff, if that's all right with you," said Faustino. He lifted his finger from the button and the tape began to run. "Tell me about where you grew up."

"At the edge of the world. That's how it seemed to me. A red dusty road came from somewhere and passed through our town. Then it went on to the edge of the forest, where the men were cutting down the trees. Beyond the edge of the forest there was nothing, or that is what my father told me. He meant that the forest seemed to go on for ever from there. Each day, at dawn, a number of trucks stopped at the top of the town where the men were waiting. My father was one of them, and he climbed up into a truck and went off to work, cutting down the trees. He sometimes came home and told us stories, like how his team had cut down a really big one, and how the monkeys who lived in it had stayed clinging onto the top branches almost until they hit the ground, and how they then ran howling into the deeper forest with babies hanging off their bellies. I didn't know if that or any of the other stuff he told me was true or not. But I grew up listening to his stories and loving them. So perhaps, in spite of everything he did to try to stop me, it was my father who set me on the path that brought me to where I am today.

During the day, the big yellow tractors that hauled the logs back down the road growled past the town in clouds of red dust which drifted into the square, the plaza, where we played football. It was just a big patch of ground between the tin church and the café. No grass. We had games that started as soon as we were let out of school and didn't end until our fathers came back in the trucks and darkness was falling. We were all football crazy, of course.

Actually, it was not just us kids who were obsessed with football. The whole place was. The café had TV, and everyone squeezed in there to watch the big matches. The walls were covered with posters and photos – our players, German, Spanish and English players, great players and teams from the past. And after a big match, even if it was dark, even if it was raining, we would run into the plaza to replay the action, calling ourselves by the names and nicknames of the great stars: Pelé, the Grey Ghost, Little Bird, Maradona, whatever."

"And you were El Gato, the Cat," said Paul Faustino.

The big goalkeeper smiled. "Oh no. Not then," he said. "You see, I was useless. I couldn't play. The other kids could do great things with the ball. Take it out of the air on the top of the foot. Run and keep it in the air with the head, score goals with bicycle kicks, stuff like that. I could do none of this. When the ball came to me – which wasn't often, the other kids made sure of that – it always seemed to get stuck between my ankles or bounce off my knees. I had no balance – a soft tackle from a smaller kid would send me staggering like a drunken goat. I was too tall. I had long skinny arms and legs, and big clumsy hands. They called me La Cigüeña – the Stork. Which was fair enough."

Faustino was a little puzzled. "But you played in goal, surely," he said.

"No. It never occurred to me. I dreamt of being a striker, of slamming in perfect shots that brought imaginary crowds roaring to their feet. We all did. Besides, there were two big strong kids who were always the goalies. So I just got pushed further and further out to the edge of the game. And even then, if the ball happened to come towards me, the nearest player on my side would yell 'Leave it!' and collect the ball instead. One day I played for two hours and didn't touch the ball once, except for when it hit me on the backside by chance. That was the day I decided to give up football. I was thirteen."

"All the same," Faustino said dryly, "you've played a game or two since."

The goalkeeper smiled again. "Yes, my retirement was a bit premature, as it turned out. But I never played in the plaza again. And it was giving up football that made me a footballer."

"You've lost me," Faustino said. "What does that mean, 'giving up football made me a footballer'?"

"I was learning nothing in the plaza. If I hadn't quit,

11

I wouldn't have gone into the forest, which is where I learnt everything."

"I get the feeling," Faustino sighed, "that I'm not going to get answers by asking questions. OK, so tell me the story. Tell me how a non-player passes the time in a foot-ball-crazy jungle town."

"At first I didn't know what to do with myself. Without the game, the afternoons seemed to last for ever, and there was nothing, absolutely *nothing*, to do. My mother and grand-mother didn't want me hanging around, and in those days there was no way that a teenage boy could be seen doing work around the house. I could read, of course, but the only books in town were in the school. Somehow I had to fill my afternoons for the two long years before I could climb onto the truck with my father and go to work."

Faustino leant towards the microphone and said, "Tell me a little about your family, Gato. What was your house like?"

"Like all the others. No, a bit bigger, because we had Nana, Father's mother, living with us, and Father built a kind of extension sticking out from the back wall. He always called it 'the new rooms', even though he had made it when I was five years old and Mother was expecting the next child, my sister. Really, those rooms were just little cubicles. My mother and father slept in one of them. Nana and my sister slept in another, and I had the third, smallest one. My grandmother snored very loudly, and the walls were just sheets of board. It sometimes drove us crazy. Except for my sister, strangely enough. Even though she slept just across the room from Nana, the snoring didn't bother her. She used to say that if Nana stopped snoring, she would never be able to sleep. My grandmother's snores were the rhythm of my sister's rest.

But our house was the same as all the others, basically. White-painted concrete blocks and a tin roof. The whole town had been built very quickly – overnight, Nana used to say. They bulldozed the road into the forest then hacked out a space and put up these houses for the tree-cutters. The main part of our house was one room with a makeshift kitchen at one end. Some families cooked on a wood stove like a barbecue, but we had a cooker with bottled gas. We got water from a pipe which we shared with five other families. My father covered our tin roof with leaves and branches to reduce the heat, but in the hot season it was still like living under a grill. In those months we lived and ate out of doors. My father slept in a hammock slung between a pepper tree and a hook driven into the wall of the house."

El Gato stopped speaking. He was staring at the gold trophy in front of him, and Paul Faustino could see two reflections of it glittering in the goalie's eyes.

"I used to have this fantasy," Gato said next. "May I tell you?"

Faustino smiled and made a willing gesture. "Of course."

"I used to imagine winning this." Gato circled a fingertip on the top of the globe. "And taking it home with me. At night, secretly. Unannounced. My father would be asleep in his hammock. I would lay the Cup gently on his chest and put his hands around it. So that when he woke up he would find himself holding the greatest prize in the world. And I would watch his face."

"And now that you have the Cup," said Faustino, "you can make this fantasy come true. Is that what you will do? Can I come with you? Would you mind if we took photographs?"

"Unfortunately," Gato said, "my father is dead."

Faustino was silent for several moments – out of respect or, perhaps, disappointment. Then the keeper removed his hand and his gaze from the gold trophy and said, "What were we talking about?"

Gently, Faustino reminded him. "About what you did when you gave up football."

EL GATO TOOK a sip of water and said, "When I gave up football I realized something. I realized that the world I had been living in was *low*."

"Low?" Faustino repeated. "What does that mean, Gato?"

"I was tall, as I said. I could stand in my bedroom and touch the timbers that held up the roof. In the schoolroom, we looked down – down at our books, down at the tips of our pencils, down at the page of the atlas that showed our country and the empty space where our town was. And in the plaza, in the games, I watched feet. I was always looking down. I think it is true to say that I hardly ever looked up until I stopped playing football."

"And when you stopped playing football and looked up, what did you see?"

"Sky and trees. Sky and trees. Very simple. You find this

hard to believe, perhaps, but I had never thought about this before. I'd never really thought about the fact that I was living in a small space hacked from the jungle. I hadn't realized that if the trees had not been cleared to make room for our town, I would never have seen the stars. The forest trees climb and occupy the whole sky, you know. In the forest, the sky is a rare thing.

Because I no longer played the game, I found myself lying on my back looking up at the sky and watching how the clouds and then the stars disappeared into the forest, how the forest covered and swallowed everything. I understood that I was *surrounded*. And I wanted to get out. I think I began wandering into the forest to see if there was a way out of it. And because there was nothing else to do.

You need to understand that the forest, or the jungle, call it what you like, was always trying to remove our little town. It would send long green fingers across the cleared spaces to climb up walls and lift the roofs off our houses. On Sundays, after church, my father would walk around the walls of our house with a machete, chopping off the jungle's fingers to keep it safe in its leafless space. At least once a month something would sneak out of the jungle and take one of our chickens. Before we went to sleep at night, Father would carry a torch and a heavy stick around the house, checking for snakes. And because my father and the other men and women of the town spent so much time beating back the jungle, there was a small belt of half-tamed land around the houses, a strip of struggling bushes with paths pushed through them, paths our neighbours walked. But only in the daylight.

One day, I decided to walk through the safe area around the houses and go into the dark high forest. I was not particularly brave. I was bored, and I was lonely. That is why I went. I walked along the paths where the chickens and the pigs scratched around for food until I came to the gloomy wall of the forest.

There were paths that went in there. I was only a child, of course, so I didn't understand that these paths had been made by animals, not people. I would follow them until they disappeared, until they vanished among the complicated roots of trees and the thick carpet of leaves and ferns. I met glittering insects, and glistening frogs, and sometimes brilliant-feathered parrots; and I learnt the difference between the harmless screaming of these animals and the dark silence that crept into the jungle when a jaguar was near by. And when I lay down to sleep in the black heat of my room, my dreams were of this new and fascinating darkness.

As I said, I was not brave. I was just as scared of the forest as everyone else was. Things I could not see would scuttle away from my feet. Things would crash through the leaves above my head. Sometimes I would cry aloud in fright. And the forest has a smell, too – a sort of thick, sweet, rotten smell that makes the air difficult to breathe.

The light is dim and green. Where the sun does break through, its light is broken up by the leaves into patches and freckles of brightness and shadow so that it's often hard to make out the shape of things."

Paul Faustino shuddered theatrically. "Not my kind of place," he said.

"No," Gato said, trying to imagine his elegant friend coping with the discomforts of the jungle. "And there were plenty of people who thought it was no place for me, either. Our town was small and talkative, and it was not long before my family heard of my little expeditions into the wilderness. My father was stern. He knew how dangerous the jungle was, he said, because it was his job to fight it. He told me of plants that scratch and fill the stratches with a poison that spreads through your body and kills you in an hour. He told me of how a man working with him had stepped into the forest to pee and never been seen again. He told me of secret tribes of wild, painted forest people who stole children away and ate them. My mother cried and prayed aloud while he told me these things.

But when it came to horror stories about the jungle, no one could compete with Nana. Ah, the things she told me! In the rivers and pools there were anacondas, giant snakes. If you looked into the water, Nana said, they would hypnotize you with the cold blue fire in their eyes, then rise up out of the water, crush you to death and swallow you whole. She told me, shuddering, about the *ya-te-veo* tree, which had long, living, evil roots covered in thorns bigger than knife blades. If you walked anywhere near them these roots would seize you and nail you to the tree-trunk, and there you would die a long and terrible death while the tree drank the blood that flowed from your wounds. There were giant spiders, she said, that leapt onto your face and suffocated you with their thick hairy bodies. There were worms, she said, that burrowed into your toes and worked up through your body until they reached your brains and ate them, so that you went crazy before you died. She had a great imagination, my grandmother. She should have been a writer for the American movies. But the *worst* thing, she said – and she crossed herself – was that the Waiting Dead lived in the darkness of the forest. I was puzzled. And also interested.

'Do you mean ghosts, Nana?'

She shrugged. 'Ghosts, zombies, they are called many things.'

'Why do you say they are waiting, Nana? What are they waiting for?'

'They are waiting for the thing that can make them truly dead, so that their hungry spirits can be peaceful. Until they get it, they have to go on waiting, searching. Maybe for ever. A terrible thing.' She shivered dramatically.

'I still don't understand,' I said. 'What is this thing that the Waiting Dead are waiting for?'

'Something they wanted very much when they were

alive, and never had. They cannot properly die because they still hunger for this thing.'

Crazy stuff, of course, but I was fascinated by it. 'But what kind of thing might this be?' I persisted.

'It could be anything,' Nana said. 'Maybe there is one waiting out there who always wanted a son. A tall handsome thirteen-year-old son.'

Then she crossed herself again and hugged me. 'No,' she said. 'God forgive me for saying such a thing.'

But, despite everything, I went into the forest again and again. Why? Well, as I said, there was nothing else to do, and nowhere else to go. And I saw wonderful things. Shimmering green humming-birds smaller than butterflies, a family of tiny emerald frogs living in less than a cupful of water, moths with wings as clear as coloured glass, like little pieces of the church window, golden millipedes longer than my arm tracking through the leaf-rubbish of the forest floor. I saw beetles that looked like flowers and flowers that looked like beetles."

El Gato caught the expression on Faustino's face and laughed. "This nature stuff really appeals to your romantic imagination, doesn't it, Paul?"

"Oh, absolutely," Faustino said, flicking unsuccessfully at his cigarette lighter. "Can't get enough of it. Us city boys just love creepy-crawlies and weird flowers. Do go on."

"OK, Paul, enough. But listen – when you write this up, you're going to have to grit your teeth and somehow get across to the readers the magic of the forest. It's important, really important. You'll see why, I promise."

"I'll do my best," Faustino said, and, seeing the sceptical look on the footballer's face, lifted his hands in a gesture of surrender and said it again.

"OK, Paul, I trust you. Anyway, despite everything my family said, I started to go further and further in. Looking back now, I think I was looking for something *in* the forest, rather than a way *out* of it."

"And you found it, this thing you were looking for?"

It was darker now, and the city below Faustino's office was a jazzy dance of neon signs and traffic. The big footballer went to the window and looked down at it all, spreading his large hands on the glass. "No," he said. "It found me."

GATO TURNED AWAY from the city and said, "It hap-pened on the day I broke the one rule I had made for myself. Like I said, I used to follow tracks into the forest until they ran out, and then I would either turn round and follow them back or maybe explore a little way off the path. But never more than just a little way, so that I always knew where the track was. The one thing I was truly afraid of was getting lost, of being lost in there when the darkness came in. So that was the rule I set myself – never lose sight of the track. And then one day I broke this rule. I don't know why. I think perhaps I saw a bigger patch of sunlight through the undergrowth ahead of me, and my curiosity was stronger than my common sense. Whatever. Anyway, I shoved through the foliage, clambering over a fallen trunk that was soft with rot and moss, and pushed aside a curtain of thick fleshy leaves. And found myself in an open space.

You probably don't think this remarkable. But if you knew the jungle, you would find it hard to believe me, because an open space in the jungle is not possible. Something, *anything*, will occupy any space where it can find light to live and grow. Yet here was this clearing, and it was covered in grass. Yes, grass. Short grass. *Turf.* Impossible. Absolutely impossible. I walked out onto this grass very slowly, far more alarmed by this clearing than by any plant or creature I had met in the jungle itself. And it was very, very *quiet*. The whirring and clicking and calling and screeching of the forest had become blurred and then silent.

I was in a space that was about ninety metres long and maybe half as wide, and I had walked out of the forest at a point about halfway down its length. I looked at first to my left, and saw how the clearing ended in a dense shadowy wall of trees. Then I looked to my right. And froze.

Standing there, with its back to the trees, was a goal. A football goal. Two uprights and a crossbar. With a net. A net fixed up like the old-fashioned ones, pulled back and tied to two poles behind the goal. My brain stood still in my head. I could hear the thumping of my blood. I must have looked like an idiot, my eyes mad and staring, my mouth hanging open. Eventually I found the nerve to take a few steps towards this goal, this quite impossible goal. The woodwork was a silvery grey, and the grain of the wood was open and rough. Weathered, like the timber of old boats left for years on a beach. It shone slightly. The net had the same colour, like cobweb, and thin green plant tendrils grew up the two poles that supported it.

It seemed to take an age, my whole life, to walk into that goalmouth. When I got there I put out my hands and held the net. It was sound and strong, despite its great age. I was completely baffled, and stood there, my fingers in the mesh of the net and my back to the clearing, trying, and failing, to make sense of all this.

And then my fingers began to tremble, and then my legs, because I was suddenly certain that I was not alone. I do not know how I forced myself to turn round.

And here I find the words difficult, Paul. I could say that he stepped out of the trees, but that is not quite right. He moved into the clearing, that is true, but he did not seem to be solid until he stopped moving. You know how sometimes you get bad TV reception, and there is a kind of shadow that follows the picture, so that things seem to happen twice? It was a bit like that: I watched him move and saw him standing still at the same time.

He was a goalkeeper, but I had never seen a kit like the one he was wearing. He wore a high-necked knitted sweater. Green, like the forest. And long shorts made of heavy-looking cotton. I was immediately interested in his boots, which were high, clumsy-looking, made of brown leather and laced in a complicated way – the laces went over and under his foot, and were tied at the back of his ankles.

He wore an old-fashioned cloth cap with a big peak which cast a deep shadow over the upper part of his face so that I couldn't see his eyes. Perhaps because of this, his face had no expression whatsoever. Under his left arm he had a football – not the kind we played with in the plaza, but a brown one, made of leather, with a pattern like bricks.

There we stood, facing each other. All I could hear was my heart pumping. What I wanted, most of all, was not to be there. It was like having a nightmare and knowing that you are having a nightmare, and that all you have to do is wake up, but you can't wake up. I was trembling like a leaf in the rain. I must have moved, made some sign of running back the way I had come, because he spoke then. The Keeper spoke, and that *really* scared me.

You know how American movies get dubbed in this country, Paul? The actors speak and someone else's voice says the words in our language, and the actor's lips don't quite match the soundtrack. The way the Keeper spoke was like that. Out of sync. The words seemed to take a long time to reach me.

And what he said was: *'There. Your place. You belong there.'*

So of course I flipped. Maybe I screamed, I don't know. But the next thing I knew I was plunging through that curtain of leaves and hurling myself over that rotting mossy tree-trunk and running stumbling back to where I hoped, prayed, my house was.

That night, in my hot dark room, I shook like I had the fever. I dreamt it all again and again: the clearing, just as I had found it, but bathed in light as if a million electric lamps burned down onto it. A light so brilliant that it drained colour from everything, and the only shadow was the one that hid half the Keeper's face below the peak of his cap. The clearing, the goalmouth, the trees, were all silver beneath a black sky. In the dream I looked up at the silver trees and they were swirling wildly, as if in a great wind. And the wind had a voice, a huge whispering voice that said: *There. Your place. You belong there.*

I pulled myself out of this dream I don't know how many times during that night. But each time I fell back into sleep I was there again, in that windswept silver-lit clearing with the Keeper. I could not escape him. And those same words, over and over again: *There. Your place. You belong there.* Sometimes the wind spoke them, sometimes he did, his mouth moving before the words came. Towards dawn, exhausted, I dreamt the dream one last time and heard the voice again. Except that this time it was not the voice of the wind, and it was not the voice of the Keeper. It was my own voice, saying: *Here. My place. I belong here.*

I was a wreck the next morning. Mother took one look at me and dismissed the idea of school. She made me strong tea and put me into Father's hammock in the shade of the pepper tree.

In the afternoon I went down to the plaza to watch the

game. I sat on the veranda of the café next to old Uncle Feliciano, Nana's brother, the one with the crooked leg. He bought me a Coke, paying for it with a filthy crumpled note that he found somewhere inside his many layers of ancient clothes. Then he rested his chin on his hands, which were cupped over the handle of his walking stick. We watched the game: the arguments, the calls, the appeals to the invisible referee, the goalscorers falling to their knees with their arms raised like the players on TV.

After a while, Uncle Feliciano spoke, without turning his head to me. 'Why don't you play?'

I shrugged. 'I don't feel so good. A touch of the fever, I think.'

'It's not that,' said Uncle Feliciano. 'You don't play no more. You haven't played for a long time. I noticed.'

I said nothing.

'Maria says you go into the forest.'

It took me a moment to remember that my grandmother's name was Maria.

'Sometimes,' I said.

'And I can imagine what Maria says about that,' Uncle Feliciano said, still watching the square. 'All those nightmare stories of hers. She has told you those?'

'Yes,' I said.

The old man made a crackled noise that might have been laughter.

'Old women,' he said. 'They have not many pleasures.

One of them is to frighten young boys.'

Then he did turn to look at me, and he took a hand from his stick and stroked the side of my face with a bent finger.

'You have seen something,' he said.

I concentrated on my bottle of Coke.

'No,' I said.

'Yes,' he said. He looked back at the game, but he was not watching it. 'You have seen something in the forest. I can tell. Listen to me. You think I am an old fool. Maybe I am. But I bought the Coke and you can listen to me until you have finished it.'

I had about three mouthfuls left in the bottle.

'It is about respect,' the old man said. '*Respect.* You know what this word means?'

'I think so, Uncle,' I said.

'I think you do not,' he said. 'I did not know what respect was when I was your age. But let us agree that you do know. So, if you respect the forest, there is nothing, *nothing*, in there that will harm you. Believe me.'

He made a gesture like someone clearing cobwebs from a path in front of him. 'All this,' he said, 'this plaza, this metal church, the game here, all this is here only because the forest allows it. Your father thinks that the forest can be beaten, cut back. Does he still go around the house on Sundays with his machete?'

I smiled. 'Yes, Uncle, he does.'

'Ha! He is fighting a losing battle and he thinks he can

win it. Does he think that when he and his friends have cut down the whole forest there will be a beautiful world for him to live in? A world of red dust to be happy in?'

I had one mouthful of Coke left. I lifted the bottle to my lips. The old man reached across and stopped my arm.

'Trust the forest,' he said. 'Respect it. You are not exploring it. It is exploring you.'

I finished the Coke."

"So I WENT back in, just as I knew I would.

I didn't look, but I knew that the moment I stepped into the clearing the Keeper appeared too. I walked, as steadily as I could, to the goalmouth. I don't know why. Perhaps I thought I would feel safer there. I turned to face him. He was exactly the same: invisible eyes and the old leather ball in the crook of his arm. Motionless.

We stood facing each other as before. Then he began to walk towards me. My mouth went completely dry. The desire to run away was almost too strong to resist. Then he stopped, about twenty yards from me. He put the ball on the ground and stepped a few paces back from it. Somehow I knew what I was expected to do, so I did it. I bent my knees, lifted my shoulders, spread my arms. I was awkward, I know, trying to fill that goalmouth. I knew who I was: Cigüeña, the Stork.

Nothing happened.

'What are you waiting for?' I was amazed to hear my own voice.

Then he moved in that way of his, like one photograph melting into another. He struck the ball with incredible force. It went past me with a noise like a gasp. The net bulged and hissed, and the ball rolled slowly back out of the goal past my feet. Which were frozen to the spot. I had not moved at all.

The Keeper's lips moved out of time with his words. 'What were you waiting for?'

My head buzzed with questions, and I somehow stammered them out.

'Who are you? What do you want? What do you want me to do?'

And then I found the right question: 'Why have you brought me here?'

The Keeper walked towards me then. My whole body flinched, but I stayed there. He stooped and picked up the ball with one hand.

'To keep goal,' he said. 'You know that.'

'I do not know that,' I said. 'I am not a goalie. I cannot play football. I have stopped playing football.'

'Yes,' he said, 'you stopped so that you could start to learn. We have a lot of work to do. Let us begin.'"

El Gato put the tips of his long fingers together and rested his hands on the table. "Two years, Paul. Almost every afternoon for two years. And at the end of that time I knew pretty much everything I know now. OK, I have played professionally for fourteen years, two of them in Italy, and I am stronger and maybe a little faster than I was back then. But everything I know, really *know*, about football and keeping goal I learnt in the forest."

Faustino could not think of anything to say, which was a new experience for him. He looked sideways at the goalkeeper, wondering if perhaps this story was a complicated joke of some sort. But Gato's face was quite settled and without mischief. So the writer cleared his throat and said, "And how did it work, this, er, training regime in the jungle? Was it just the two of you?"

"Well, yes and no. I discovered that there are many teachers in the forest. I will come to that. But on that first day the Keeper began by crushing me – completely wiping me out. He simply put shot after shot past me, saying nothing, just placing the ball on the grass, stepping back one or two paces, fading slightly, then coming back into focus and shooting into the net. I jumped and twitched in the goalmouth like a hooked fish, but never once got so much as a finger to the ball. My eyes filled with sweat and tears of frustration. After a while I stopped trying to block his shots and just stood there between the posts watching him. And when I stopped, he stopped too.

'Good,' the Keeper said. 'You have already learnt to keep still. Stay there and tell me where this next shot is going.'

'How? What do you mean?'

'Watch me, boy. Not the ball, me. And when my foot hits the ball, tell me where the shot is going. High, low, left, right. Shout it. Don't move, don't try to stop it, just shout out where the shot is going.'

He placed the ball on the grass and stepped back. I watched him take two quick paces, and as he struck the ball I yelled, 'High, right!' The ball flew into the top corner of the net above my right shoulder.

'Again,' the Keeper ordered. I rolled the ball to him. While it was still moving, he dropped his right shoulder slightly and shot at me with his left foot.

'Low, right!' I screamed. The ball streaked into the net to my right, two centimetres above the grass. I picked the ball out of the net and turned to face him.

'The hard thing,' he said, 'is to know how we know something. Explain how you knew where those shots were going.'

'I didn't know,' I said. 'I just guessed.'

The Keeper put his hands on his hips. 'Give me the ball,' he said. 'And let us test your guesswork some more.'

He put ten more shots past me and I called them correctly eight times.

'You are reading the body,' he said. 'When a player shoots at your goal, he will do things which tell you where he wants the ball to go. He will lean slightly to the left or the right to put weight into the shot, and his own weight onto one foot or the other. He will drop one shoulder, and almost always his shot will be in a line with that shoulder. Most players cannot help glancing, for a fraction of a second, at where they intend to send the ball. A right-footed player may fake a shot, but if he lifts his right arm up and back, he will then shoot. These things can be learnt. But an instinct for them is a gift. As I thought, you have this gift.'

I was pleased with myself. For just a few seconds, because the Keeper then said, 'But this gift is nothing in itself. It does not make you a keeper.' He put the ball on the ground a few yards out from the middle of the goal. The place where the penalty spot would have been.

'Now you have to beat me,' he said. He walked past me into the goalmouth, moving in the blurred way I was slowly becoming used to. I shrank away from him as we passed.

I was no great shot, Paul. Like I said, I was a tall skinny kid, and I was never sure where my balance was. But I had listened to what the Keeper had told me. I thought about how to disguise my shot. I decided to take it with the inside of my right foot and put it low to the Keeper's left. I didn't look at him, or at where I was sending the shot. I looked only at the ball. I hit it well. And when I looked up, the ball was in the Keeper's hands, and he was no longer in the middle of the goal. He had somehow, magically, arrived at exactly where I had aimed the shot.

He threw the ball out to me. 'Again,' he said.

And this time, just as I made the shot, he lifted his right arm and the ball flew into his hand as if I had aimed it there. He threw the ball out to me.

'Again,' he said.

Time after time, and every time, he drew my shots to him. He seemed to make no effort at all. He was simply, easily, in the place where I did not want him to be.

'You are reading me,' I said.

'No. I am telling you where I want the ball, and you are obeying. Let me tell you something. When there is a penalty kick, most people think that the penalty taker is in control. But they are wrong. The penalty taker is full of fear, because he is expected to score. He is under great pressure. He has many choices to make, and as he places the ball and walks back to make his run, his mind is full of the possibility of failure. This makes him vulnerable, and it makes the keeper very powerful.'

'Are you saying that the keeper can decide where the penalty shot goes?'

'Yes. Great keepers can do this. But as I said, you have a long way to go. For one thing, you do not know what your eyes can do. Come here tomorrow, and I will teach you to see.'"

"I did go back, of course, that next afternoon, and he was standing there, as before, with his back to the dark wall of the forest. Waiting.

I walked into the clearing. Now it seemed less strange to do so. I went to the ancient silvery goalmouth and stood between the posts and looked at him.

'No,' he said. 'Come and stand here.'

I did not want to. I was still very, very afraid of being close to him. I had seen his huge hands seize the football, and my grandmother's superstitions had taken root in my imagination.

I stood a short distance from him. The shadow on his face was as dark as ever and he did not seem to have any eyes at all.

'Look,' he said. 'What do you see?'

I had no idea what he meant me to say. I looked down the length of the clearing at the goal and the grey net hanging from it, and behind the net the shades of green deepening into the forest.

'What?' I asked. 'I see the goal. Is there something else?'

'Try again,' he said. 'I ask too much of you, perhaps. Look at the crossbar.'

This time I saw something, some sort of very small animal, moving along the bar. From that distance, it was just a reddish-brown blur without edges or detail.

The Keeper lifted his face. I thought I caught two glints of light where his eyes should have been. 'Look at the sky,' he said. 'Just there, look. What do you see?'

The sky was all one colour, something like bright

metal. It was hard to look up into it. I narrowed my eyes and saw a hawk hovering, its wingtips spread, holding the air, striped tail tilted downwards. Tiny from where we stood.

'Now,' the Keeper said, 'what does the hawk see?'

I shaded my eyes with my hand, and as I did so I felt a kind of lurch, as if the space around me had shifted somehow. The Keeper repeated his question, but this time his voice seemed to come from somewhere inside my own head. *'What does the hawk see? Look!'*

And I saw through the eyes of the hawk. Far below me, the emerald-green regular shape of the clearing was like a mistake in the infinite forest. I looked down on it as if through a powerful telescope, a telescope focused on just a few centimetres of the grainy crossbar of the goal, which I saw in fantastic detail. And something moved into the focus of the hawk's eyes. A mouse of some sort. Or a rat. A little mammal with small flickering eyes, large ears, long tail. Scuttling along the crossbar, stopping now and then, sniffing the air anxiously. I felt its fear, and something else, too; there was a connection between the hunter and the victim. It was like a thread that tied them together, like the string of a kite attached to the hand of the child flying it. The instant I realized this, the hawk folded its wings into itself and followed the invisible thread downwards at relentless speed, spreading itself at the last possible moment, breaking its fall at the second its claws daggered into its prey. And then it was back in the air, the corpse hanging from its feet.

I lowered my hand from my eyes and was back on the grass in the clearing with the Keeper.

'Get in the goal,' he said, and walked the ball away from me. He was maybe twenty-five yards out when he stopped and turned to face me. I stood in the centre of the goal in a state of shock. The Keeper had shifted the limits of my world, or maybe simply rubbed them out. Now, as if nothing out of the ordinary had happened, he was preparing to take a free kick at me.

It was a beautiful free kick. It went off to my left round a wall of imaginary players, then turned and dipped towards the top left-hand corner of the goal. But I *knew* it would go there. I could see the path it was on. It was as if the ball was flying along an invisible thread that was attached to my hand. I took off like a bird and reached out to it, and I palmed it over the bar. My legs were everywhere, and I landed in an ugly heap, almost crashing into the upright.

When I got to my feet the Keeper was standing at the spot from which he had taken the kick.

'Good,' he said. 'At least you can see.'"

EL GATO EXCUSED himself and set off for the men's room, which – and this was another source of grief to Faustino – was at the far end of the seventh floor. The journalist leant back in his chair and considered the options. The first and most obvious was that the world's greatest goalkeeper was barking, moonstruck mad. This idea was itself crazy; the man's calmness, his absolute control over stress, was legendary. On the other hand, Faustino reminded himself, nutters were sometimes like that: completely normal to all appearances, calm as milk until someone or something hit whatever hidden switch or lever it was that sent them into some other orbit. But no. He'd known the man for years, and if there'd been any sign of buried craziness he'd have spotted it. Besides, Gato's tone of voice was so matter-of-fact, with none of the passion of the fantasist. OK, then; this jungle story was an elaborate, carefully thought-through wind-up. But what for? If this was all bullshit, and it was printed under Paul Faustino's name, Paul Faustino's credibility – and his job – would go down the pan. Was that it? Did Gato have some reason to destroy the reputation of someone he called a friend? The thought made Faustino reach for his cigarettes. Had he ever done anything, written anything about the man that deserved this kind of vengeance? At panic speed, Faustino ran through the history of their friendship and found nothing.

So: rule out madness, rule out deliberate, systematic lying... What was left? Faustino had no idea. There was clearly nothing to do other than let the goalkeeper talk this thing out, and then review the situation. Take advice, maybe. But from whom? Was there anyone who could back up this wild story? Had Gato told all this to anyone else? Now *there* was an interesting thought...

Faustino sighed and lit up. One thing was certain: this was not going to be the one-hour interview he'd planned on. It looked like a long night ahead.

The goalkeeper came back into the office and sat down. He regarded Faustino silently. Faustino met his eyes and had the very uncomfortable feeling that Gato knew exactly what he had been thinking. Neither man spoke. Eventually Faustino simply leant forward and pressed the *record* button on the machine. The goalkeeper began to speak again. That same measured tone of voice.

"As the days and weeks went by my moods changed like the sky. Sometimes I would come out of the forest really high, you know? Exhilarated. At other times I would be almost in despair, certain that I would never master the skills the Keeper was trying to teach me. Very often I was lost in thought, rerunning the afternoon in my head. I became distant, I suppose. So my family became more and more worried. My mother was particularly anxious. When she asked what I had been doing, I told her I had been 'exploring'. To try to reassure her, I told her about the things I had seen: flowers, animals, insects. But I had to make a lot of this stuff up because, in fact, I no longer took much notice of what I saw in the jungle. My travels into the forest now had only one purpose: to get as quickly as possible to the clearing and the Keeper. All the same, my mother clung to the notion that I had some sort of scientific interest; and this is what she told my father. He was uneasy, but made a joke of it, and for a while he called me 'the Explorer'. 'And what did the Explorer discover today?' he would ask when we all sat down to eat. Then I would talk about beetles and plants and so on.

Looking back now, Paul, I find it surprising that my father knew very little about these things himself. Not just surprising, but sad, too. He was in the forest every day of his working life, but seemed to know so little about it. When he spoke about his work, his stories were mostly about the men he worked with. When he spoke about the forest, his talk was about the difficulties and successes he had met while cutting it down. He was expert at calculating the weight and balance of a tree, and the direction in which it would fall if the saws made the right cuts. When he looked at a tree, he saw what it might be turned into: houses, boats, furniture, telephone poles, paper. Money."

Faustino did not miss the faint bitterness that had seeped into the footballer's voice.

"But as you said earlier, my friend, that was his job. Surely it's a good thing that he did it well."

"Of course, of course." A touch of impatience in Gato's voice. "I'm not saying that my father was a vandal. All I'm saying is that it's sad and strange that those men like my father who lived and worked in the forest knew nothing about it. And I know they didn't, because I worked alongside them for a while."

"Did you?"

"Yes, but I'm getting ahead of the story here. I'll come to that. So, anyway, I encouraged my mother to believe that I was the budding naturalist. The problem was, it got harder and harder to make stuff up. That's the trouble with lies: you have to remember them all, tell the same ones every time, so that you don't get caught out."

"I wouldn't know," said Faustino.

"Of course not, Paul. You're a journalist."

Faustino put on a big innocent smile.

"So," Gato continued, "I had to do some work on this

cover story of mine. I had to begin taking notice of what I saw on my way to the clearing and back, so that I could tell my mother something new each evening. I started to bring things back. Leaves, flowers, dead beetles in a matchbox, skins that small snakes had shed, little skulls. They didn't mean much to me. I just left them lying around. Then one Sunday my father spent the afternoon fixing up shelves in my room, and my mother proudly arranged all these bits and pieces from the forest on them. I hadn't known that she had collected and kept them. Later that week she went to the market and bought me three big notebooks, several ballpoint pens and a tin of coloured pencils. Which made my sister very envious, of course. And which made me feel trapped. Now I had to take the whole business seriously.

Most evenings, after dinner, I would sit at the table beneath the moth-flickered light and record and draw the things that I had found. At first, it drove me crazy, because what was buzzing in my head wasn't plants or insects, but football. Then, after a while, I began to enjoy doing it. For one thing, it was a way for me to calm down. And it made my mother happy, and I loved her, so that was good."

"What about your father?"

"A hard question, Paul. He was led by my mother, so if she was happy he was happy too. For a while, anyway. His problem was that he couldn't see the point of it. We lived in a logging town. The only reason the town existed was to cut trees. My father knew for a fact that when I left school I would work for the logging company. There was no alternative. In my town, boys grew into loggers, girls grew into the wives of loggers, they would have children who became either loggers or the wives of loggers, and that was that. So he didn't see the point of me becoming an expert in the ways of the forest. He thought it was unnatural. My mother had a bigger vision of the world. She had begun to imagine me as a professor, giving lectures in Rio, or New York, or Europe. Her mistake was to share these dreams with my father, when he didn't want to know. He didn't want the safe rhythms of his life upset by ambition. That's how people got hurt. So now and again he'd snap, like a rope carrying too much weight. Then there'd be shouting and tears."

"You heard them, these rows?" Faustino wanted to know.

"Oh, sure. Like I said, the walls in our house were thin. My father hadn't been thinking about arguments when he built them."

The goalkeeper went once again to the window and looked down at the city.

"I bet you," he said, "that down there, in thousands of buildings, thousands of parents are arguing about what they want their children to be. And in almost every case their children will turn out to be something their parents never even thought of. There's nothing unusual about what happened to my family. My mother and father fought the same fight that's going on down there. The only difference is that they fought the battle in the middle of the jungle."

Faustino had different thoughts about the ordinariness of what had gone on in El Gato's childhood, but he kept them to himself.

The big man returned to the table. "Can you remember what your parents wanted you to be, Paul?"

"They wanted me to be a doctor," said Faustino, lighting up again. "They are, of course, deeply disappointed."

"You must earn a lot more than the average doctor," Gato said.

"Sure I do," replied Faustino. "But that doesn't make any difference. As far as my parents are concerned, I'm just a failed doctor."

"And as far as my mother is concerned," said El Gato, "I am a failed naturalist who just happens to have won the World Cup. She still hopes that one day I will settle down and do something worthwhile."

Faustino's laugh turned into a cough, and when it had calmed, Gato said, "My parents, after many nights of fighting, came to an agreement. My mother had to admit that it would be incredibly difficult for me to have an education after I left school. The only place for someone like me to get more education was at the Advanced College, and that was in the regional capital, Puerto Madieras, which was four hundred kilometres the other side of the river. My mother had a cousin there who might be persuaded to let me live with her, but all this would cost a great deal of money. My father said that the only way to find this money would be for me to work for the logging company for maybe two years, and for the family to save all the wages I earned to pay for my time at the college. My mother agreed that this must be the way. I guess my father thought that two years of real work would put an end to all these crazy ideas.

And I heard these discussions through the wall, feeling sick with guilt. Because I knew I would never go to Puerto Madieras and learn how to become a naturalist. Because I knew that although my mother would spend hours, days, writing difficult letters to her cousin and to the college, I would never go there."

El Gato sat silently for several moments. Faustino kept quiet too. He could see that the goalkeeper had taken a long journey back in time and space to a hot troubled house, and the journalist was in no hurry to bring him back.

The tape machine made a tiny grinding sound as it recorded the silence.

"THERE WERE TIMES when I hated him," El Gato said. Faustino was confused. "What? Who, your father?"

"Of course not. *Of course not!* I'm talking about the Keeper, obviously."

The big man's sudden anger was like lightning from a clear sky and Faustino was taken aback. "Oh, right," he said. "Of course. Sorry." He waited for the other man to calm. It was an interesting process, like watching clear water sluice away a stain. When it was done, Faustino tried again.

"What made you hate him?"

"He was hard, unemotional. He didn't seem to know what praise was. He was building me, and he did it ruthlessly. Much of what we did was as you'd expect – press-ups, sit-ups, star-jumps, sprints – all in increasing repetitions as time went by. I would meet one target and instantly he would set another. And while I was working – usually when I was beginning to fade – he would suddenly blast the ball at me, and if I failed to get a hand or foot to it I would feel his icy disapproval. A few times he reduced me to tears, and when this happened he would simply turn his back and wait for me to pull myself together. He was driving me, hard. The thing that puzzled and disturbed me was that he didn't seem to be doing this for my sake, but for his. So, sometimes, I hated him."

Faustino had to ask the obvious question. "So, why didn't you quit?"

Gato seemed to find this surprising. "It never occurred to me."

"No? Not once?"

"Not once."

"OK," Faustino said.

"Besides," Gato said, "it worked, this discipline. I gained stamina. I grew stronger. My body looked less and less like a bundle of sticks tied together with string. My arms and shoulders and thighs began to fill out. My big feet started to look appropriate. I was rather pleased with myself. I began to think that sometime soon the Keeper would announce that he was pleased with me too. I should have known better."

Gato poured himself a glass of water and drank from it. Faustino was quite sure that this break in the story was meant for dramatic effect.

"One day," Gato resumed, "I came into the clearing and was surprised to see the Keeper already in the goalmouth. It was a hot, heavy afternoon. The sky was stacked up with dark grumbling clouds and the light seemed unnatural. The air in the clearing shifted uneasily from side to side. A storm was brewing not far away.

As soon as I stepped onto the turf, the Keeper moved a short distance out of the goal and told me to take his place. I stood more or less halfway between the posts. He watched me, silently, holding the ball under his arm. A glimmer of lightning flickered behind his left shoulder. I began to feel awkward, but didn't know what to say, or even if I was expected to speak. I shifted my feet, embarrassed. Then at last he spoke.

'What do you feel?'

'What do you mean?' I asked.

'It's not a difficult question. Tell me what you are feeling, standing there.'

'Um … there's a storm coming,' I said. 'And I'm wondering what you are going to make me do today. I'm wondering what you want me to say.'

'No, no,' the Keeper said. 'Those are things you are *thinking*, and that is not what I asked you. You are standing in a special place. I want you to tell me what it feels like.'

'I don't understand.'

He regarded me for a few moments.

'OK,' he said, eventually. 'I want you to walk to the goal-post to your right.'

I did.

'Now, put your hand on the post. No, face me, not the post. What do you feel?'

What I felt was the coarse grain of the wood. Was that what he meant? I didn't think so. I didn't answer his question.

'Very well. Now walk to the other post. Put your hand on it. What do you feel?'

What the hell was he expecting me to say? This was stupid.

'It's an old piece of wood,' I said. 'The other post is an old piece of wood. The bar is another old piece of wood.'

The Keeper's shadowed face told me nothing. He may have felt my impatience but clearly it was of no importance to him.

'How long did it take you to pace from one post to the other?' he demanded.

'I don't know.'

'What is the distance from one post to the other? How fast could you travel that distance? How far above your head is the bar? When you lift your arm straight up, how big is the gap between your fingertips and the bar? How far behind you is the net? Can you imagine the angle between your right post and the top-left corner of the net? How would that angle change if you stepped one pace forward?

Or two paces? If you looked at the goal from above, what shape would it be? If an opposing player were standing at the left corner of the penalty area, what would the goal look like to him?'

He hammered these questions at me and they stung me like wasps defending their nest. They were so aggressive that they brought hot tears to my eyes.

'I don't know,' I shouted. 'I don't know!'

Silence. And in that silence another flick of lightning and a grumble from the bruise-coloured clouds.

The Keeper did not react to my outburst, nor to the distress in the sky.

He said, 'If I had asked you such questions about the room you sleep in, would you have answered in the same way? Isn't it true that you know exactly the space and shape of that room? Isn't it true that you can find your way around that room in the dark as easily as in the light? Isn't it a fact that you have a very clear picture of that space in your head? More than that – don't you *feel* that space when you are in it?'

I began to understand.

'What were the first words I ever spoke to you?' the Keeper asked me.

I hadn't forgotten. Those words had galed through my dreams for an entire night. 'You said, *Your place. You belong there.*'

He nodded. 'And do you believe that, now?'

'I think so.'

'Think?' The word was hard-edged.

'I believe it. Yes, I do,' I said.

'You are a keeper?'

'Yes,' I said. 'I am a keeper.' And although I was aston-ished to hear myself say it, I did, in fact and at last, believe it. I was filled with relief, the kind of relief you feel when you give in to some irresistible force. When you know that there are no other choices to make.

The sky groaned. I looked up, and my eye was caught by a cobweb in the angle of the goalpost and the bar. It had not been there earlier. One of those flies that storms conjure up was struggling in the sticky threads of the web, and the spider was making her way swiftly towards it. Her legs were tiger-striped in bands of brown and ginger. I wondered whether I was the spider or the fly. I didn't speak the thought aloud, so I was shocked when the Keeper said, 'You are the spider. For you, the goal will not be a vulner-able place needing your protection. It will be a trap. It will be where you hunt.'

Another blue flare in the sky. The storm was almost on top of us now.

'I need to be sure that you understand me,' the Keeper said. 'Nothing is going to work if you do not own that space you are standing in. You must always be aware of how far, *exactly* how far, you are from either post. Without looking to check. You must know exactly what you have to do to get yourself into the unprotected parts of your goal. You have to understand how your body occupies the goalmouth. You must be able to imagine what your goal looks like to anyone who wants to attack it, from any direction. If you can make this goal, this web, your own, you can make any goal your own. They are all the same.'

The Keeper turned his head slightly, and the sky was bleached by what might have been the flashlight of a vast camera. The lightning arced into the forest so close to us that I could taste the electric charge in the air. When the blue light faded, it was as if night had already fallen. The first sheet of rain swept through the clearing.

Still the Keeper didn't move. Perhaps he was waiting for me to say something, but I couldn't think what that might be. At last he said, 'I think the light is not good enough for practice today. I think you might as well go home.'

By the time I got back to the house I was drenched and coated to my waist in mud. Nana took one look at me and went ballistic."

PAUL FAUSTINO SNEAKED a glance at his watch and El Gato saw him do it.

"Are you worrying about your deadline, Paul?"

"I've pretty much given up on that. This piece was meant for tomorrow's edition, but even if we'd finished, I don't think I could get this on the street tomorrow."

"Does that mean trouble for you?" Gato said.

"From my charming editor? Oh, she'll give me the Death Glare, but I'll survive it. Right now, I'm more likely to die of starvation. How about I get some coffee and sandwiches sent up? Or send out for pizza?"

"Sandwiches would be fine."

Faustino went over to the wall phone and jabbed four numbers. "Hi. Paul. Hello. Yeah, I'm good. Coffee, yes. Yeah, in a thermos jug, that'd be nice. And can you manage a big plate of sandwiches? Anything except cheese.

Great." He listened. "Yep, that's who I'm talking to. He's really here, yes. Yes, I'm sure he'll autograph a photo for you." He laughed. "Of course it's for your son, not you."

Later, the tape running again, Faustino sipped black coffee and once more pondered the mental health of his friend. It was a subject to be approached on tiptoe, if at all.

"Gato," he said, "I have to say, this isn't the kind of interview I'd imagined having with you."

"I'm sorry," Gato said.

"No, no. This is great stuff. Really. But, well ... it's a bit, er, *weird*."

The goalkeeper said nothing at all.

"What strikes me," Faustino said, "is that when you talk about these ... these *experiences* of yours, you seem, well, very calm. You must have been a very well-balanced child. If something like that had happened to me I would be in a mental hospital now."

"Well, I don't know about being well balanced. I was terrified. And that dark wet afternoon, dashing home through the storm, I thought that yes, perhaps I was going mad."

Faustino blinked, hearing the word "mad" spoken aloud, but stayed silent.

"And it was only later, much later, that I understood what the Keeper was doing."

"Which was?"

The goalkeeper leant forward and fingered the air in

front of him as if he were feeling for the right words.

"He was teaching me things, skills, of course. But he was doing something else as well. He was showing me what weakness and fear were. But in a safe place. That clearing in the jungle was like a place taken out of the real world, separate from it. Do you know what I mean? It was a place where I was allowed to feel frightened, hopeless, awkward, ashamed; but it was a place where no harm could come to me. I was protected there. I could get things wrong, but have other chances to get them right. So that, later, out there in a bigger and more dangerous world, I would be able to manage those things. He, the Keeper, was getting me ready for the life he knew I would have."

Faustino considered this. "It seems to me," he said, "that you are describing what a father should do for his son."

"I do not want to criticize my father," Gato said sharply.

"No, of course not," said Faustino. "That's not what I meant. It's just that you speak about the Keeper as if he took that role. As if he was doing certain things for you that your father couldn't do."

"Of course my father couldn't do those things for me. My father was a logger. He left in the morning dark and came home in the evening dark. His role, to use your word, was to keep his family going. And that's what he did, successfully. There are plenty of men who fail at that."

The goalkeeper was again agitated, and Faustino backed off.

He smiled. "That's true enough," he said. "I meant no disrespect to your father, my friend."

El Gato leant back in his chair. "That's OK, Paul," he said, after a pause. "Let's go on."

"Are you sure?"

"I'm sure."

"Time is stretchy stuff," El Gato said. "When you're defending a one-goal lead against a frantically attacking side, two minutes of added time can last an hour. And in the clearing with the Keeper, time didn't seem to work in the same way as it did elsewhere. It was as if we were in a glass box where the ordinary ticking of the world didn't reach us. I often came out of the forest and was surprised to find that it was an hour, perhaps more, later or earlier than I had thought; that I was out of step with the outside world. This sense I had of being in another time zone came from the Keeper, I think. He was *constant*. He didn't age or change. He'd disconnected himself, somehow. He'd escaped time. Often I felt this same freedom myself, the freedom of living untouched by the hands of the clock. Of the months marching past me, not dragging me with them. It was an illusion, of course. Looking back now, my time with the Keeper passed incredibly quickly.

By the time I was fourteen and a half, I hardly resembled the skinny kid who had crept wide-eyed into the clearing eighteen months before. At school I was still Cigüeña, the

Stork, of course. In places like that, names stick. In the café, old men called each other by nicknames they had been given half a century earlier. But there was nothing stork-like about me any more. I was taller and bigger and stronger than my father. On Saturday evenings, if he had enjoyed a couple of beers, he liked to get me to give him piggyback rides. He'd ride me around the outside of the house, whooping like a rodeo rider, until my mother appeared, laughing and scolding at the same time, to herd us inside.

And, after eighteen months, the Keeper was showing some signs of satisfaction with my progress. I remember the first time he used the words 'keepers like us'. Like *us*! I could almost feel my heart getting bigger. Usually, though, a nod of approval was the richest reward I would receive. He would force me to make a sequence of very difficult reaction saves from close range, and if I blocked every one he would say something like, 'That was almost good.' The 'almost' would sting me like a whip at first, but I got used to it. I think now that it was part of the training, denying me praise. I remember making a particularly difficult save in my second game for Unita, getting my left foot to a deflected shot, and when I watched the video the commentator called it 'a lucky stop'. Goalies get that all the time, and I've known some who let it eat into them. The Keeper taught me to expect it, and survive it.

During our second year, he spent a great deal of time

teaching me the skills of an attacking player. He himself was very good. He had somehow, somewhere, mastered the art of the free kick. I have since come up against players who were better than him at using the ball to deceive a keeper, but not many. He made me see, through the eyes of a forward, how the goalmouth looked from different angles, and how those angles might tempt one kind of shot or another. You know those clear plastic protractors you use at school to mark and measure angles? Whenever I had to lay one on a sheet of paper, I saw a goalmouth from above. While the other pupils measured the angle between one line and another, I was thinking about how a player would use his foot to send the ball along that angle. As a result, I always did badly in the geometry tests. But I learnt to measure, and calculate, and anticipate with my eyes.

We worked, the Keeper and I, on penalty kicks, over and over. I never beat him. No – I did beat him once; but only because I slipped on the grass and miscued the ball on a day when it was raining heavily.

At home, my notebooks took up more and more space on the shelves, crowding the little exhibits I had gathered on my journeys in and out of the forest. By now there were thirteen of these books. The earliest ones were filled with random, higgledy-piggledy notes, drawings, and little bits of information pinched from school textbooks. Slowly, though, they became more organized: a whole book about trees, another about moths, another about fruits and what ate them. My father stopped calling me 'the Explorer'. Now both he and Uncle Feliciano called me 'Professor'.

Uncle Feliciano came to the house once or twice a week, in the early evening. We would hear the tapping of his stick and the drag of his twisted leg on the gravel, and then he would appear round the corner of the house and sit down, with difficulty, on the chair next to mine. He would summon his sister, my grandmother, and request a glass of tea. Then he would take out his spectacles, which were held together by sticky tape and twisted paper clips, park them on his nose, and squint at my work. If I had drawn a centipede, he would count the body sections and legs, twice, to make sure I had got them right. He would criticize the colours I had used in drawings of plants. He also enjoyed teaching me the local names of the things I'd drawn.

'This one, this beetle here, we call the Bullfighter. You know why? It has one very good trick to defend itself. There are birds who like to eat him, because he is big and juicy. So when he comes up against one of these birds he pulls this big blob of red stuff, like blood but more sticky, out of his head with his front legs, and puts it on the ground next to him. For some reason, the bird goes for this red blob, not the beetle. Like a bullfighter using the red cape, you know, to distract the bull? And so the beetle escapes.'

He'd lick his finger – and I wished he wouldn't – to turn to the next page.

'Hah! Now, this one has a rude name: Stinkbum. When he is attacked, he turns round and makes a terrible smell from his back end. If you are unlucky enough to be near him when he does it, you can hear the noise it makes, like a tiny gun: *pap-ap!*'

On most of Uncle Feliciano's visits, we were not alone at the table. My mother took great pride in my books and liked to be there when Feliciano looked through them. I always felt a little flood of shame run through me when she praised my work and shared her ambitions for me with another person. But there was one evening I particularly remember, because Uncle Feliciano and I were alone at the rickety table below the bare light bulb. He flicked his dampened finger through my latest pages, but seemed less interested than usual. He closed the book and looked out at the moon.

'You know why I call you "Professor"?' he asked.

'You like to tease me, Uncle,' I said.

'No. I call you Professor to please your mother. To help you with your deceptions.'

I suddenly felt my insides clench up. I said nothing, hoping for an escape from the conversation. I knew there wouldn't be one.

'It is unusual,' he said, 'for a boy with such big hands to be good at drawing. In your hands, the pencils look like straws in a pig's fist. Your drawings are surprisingly good, considering this. And it is not just your hands. You have become big in many ways. Your family thinks this is normal. I do not. I remember the conversation we had when we watched the boys play in the plaza. You hid from me then, and you are hiding from me now. Boys do not change as much as you have changed by drawing flowers and insects. You do not get big strong hands and buffalo shoulders doing that.'

I swallowed, and said, 'I cannot help having big hands, Uncle Feliciano. It's just the way I am.'

He stared straight ahead of him at nothing in particular. I was a little shocked when he leant forward and spat into the darkness. He was angry with me because I was being dishonest with him. Or that's what I thought. So I was very surprised when he stretched out his arm and rested his hand gently on mine and spoke to me in a voice that had nothing but kindness in it.

'I am not upset in any way that there are things you cannot tell me, or things you cannot tell your family,' he said. 'People who have nothing private, who have no secrets, are empty people. I meet such people every day. This town, like all towns, is full of them. But it might be useful for you to know that you are not the first person who has discovered how to live by immersing himself in a dangerous place.'

I could think of nothing to say.

'You know now what you want to be?' Uncle's voice was very quiet now. 'You have found out? You are sure?'

'Yes,' I said.

Uncle Feliciano picked up my notebook. 'Have these anything to do with it?' he asked. 'All these books of yours your mother is so proud of?'

'No.' Saying that little word was like dragging a bone out of my throat.

He sighed. 'I won't tell her,' he said. He still held my notebook in his hand. He looked at it for quite a long time and then gave it back to me.

'I would look after these books anyway,' he said. 'You never know. Life changes. One day you might look around for these, and if they have been lost you might feel lost as well.'"

"MY FIFTEENTH BIRTHDAY was racing towards me like the shadow of a dark cloud running over the forest. I hadn't talked to the Keeper about it. I suppose he must have known that I would soon have to leave school and go to work, that these afternoons were coming to an end. But we didn't discuss it. I never admitted it to myself, but I think I was hoping that he could somehow prevent it. That he would perform some miracle to rescue me. Perhaps that was why he never spoke about it. Perhaps his silence on the subject was evidence that he had a plan.

By now, I had made that goal web my own. My eyes were good at knowing where the ball was and where it was going to be. I was big and strong and fast.

The Keeper was not satisfied.

'You are doing only one thing with your body when you make a save,' he said.

'And that is wrong?' I asked the question resentfully; I had made a number of good saves from difficult positions that afternoon.

'Not exactly,' he said. 'That is what good keepers do. But it is not good enough for you.'

'I don't understand.' How many times had I said that to him? And how many times had he been patient with my ignorance?

'A good keeper,' he said, 'gives all his body to making the save. Every muscle, every nerve, goes into the save. You do that. But it is not enough.'

'Why not?'

'Because a save, even a very good save, does not always *end* anything. You may reach a ball that should be impossible to reach, but that does not mean your job is finished. You could get injured, and you have to know how to protect yourself from that. And the ball may remain in play. So, while your body is flying through the air, even at the moment when you know you will get to the shot, even at the moment when you are congratulating yourself for getting to it, your body should be adjusting itself for what might happen next. This has nothing to do with *thinking*. It's important that you understand this. It is not a brain thing we are talking about here. Your body must know what to do. Your body must know what to do *by itself*.'

'How is that possible?' I said, feeling lost. 'My body can only do what I tell it to do. You have taught me to believe that I can make my body do what I want it to do. You are confusing me.'

The Keeper was silent for several moments. I began to fidget. I had never liked these silences.

Then he said, 'Instinct. I am sorry that I cannot think of a simpler word for it. Come, give me the ball.'

He took it out to a position about thirty-five yards down our pitch, in line with my left post.

'Here is the situation,' he instructed me. 'I am a midfield player for the other side. Looking towards your goal, I see that one of your defenders is out of position, so that for just a moment there are three of my players against two of yours. I send a long, high ball, a good one, which goes over the heads of my attackers so that they will be facing your goal when they run onto it. I'm aiming at the penalty spot. One of your defenders might be able to head it clear. What do you do?'

This wasn't difficult. 'Defensive headers are always risky,' I said. 'So I scream like hell for the ball and go out and take it.'

'Very well,' the Keeper said. 'Do it.'

He sent the pass exactly as he had described it. I knew that he would put some backspin on it, to deaden the bounce when it landed in my penalty area. I came roaring out of the goalmouth, jumped well, took the ball cleanly, high, pulled it down onto my chest and landed, well balanced, facing up the clearing. Nothing wrong with that,

I thought. I looked at the Keeper, pleased with myself.

'You put yourself in danger, collecting the ball that way.'

'I do?' I said. 'How?'

'You show too much of yourself to attacking players. Your speed is good and your jumping is good, but you always have the front of your body facing players coming in at you. This makes it easier for you to get hurt. And it makes it easier for you to be obstructed. Understand that when you are making a catch like that, there is a dangerous moment. That is when you are high in the air, with your hands on the ball, but before you get it down to your body and under control. Opposing players will be very close to you, jumping at you with their arms high, and if you lose balance at that moment you may lose the ball, even though you have big strong hands.'

I understood this. 'So what should I be doing?'

'Your body must turn so that it meets oncoming players with the shoulder and the hip, not the chest and stomach.'

'Show me,' I said.

We changed places, and I sent in the long pass, not as well as he had done, but well enough. From a standing start he came out of the goal like a tiger, in great strides: no more than four of them before he leapt. At the instant he took the ball, his body swivelled; by the time the ball had been clutched to his chest he was descending sideways, left shoulder down, weight thrown forward. I would not like to have been in his way. He looked as though he could have smashed through a brick wall. His leading left foot touched the turf first. As soon as both feet were grounded he was in a half-crouch, the ball held slightly away from his body, so that he was perfectly balanced to make either a long throw or a kick.

It seemed so easy and natural that I thought I must have missed something.

'Again?' I needed to be sure he hadn't done something too quickly for me to see.

'Very well,' the Keeper said, and rolled the ball out to me.

This time I pitched the ball a little shorter, so that he had further to go to reach it. It made no difference. Again, the tigerish run and leap, the hands behind the ball when he caught it, the pivot in the air, the shoulder-first descent, the landing in perfect balance and readiness. And this time an overarm throw the instant his feet touched the ground. The ball flew true to me and I took it on my chest.

'OK.' I trotted over to the goalmouth while he went to the ball.

He sent the long pass to exactly the same spot as before. I took the ball high in the air, my hands well positioned. I pulled it down to me and swung the balance of my body sideways as the Keeper had done. I immediately lost control of my legs. My hips were out of line with my shoulders and didn't know what to do. I was still trying desperately to get my weight in the right place when I hit the turf. To save myself from injury I got my left hand to the ground and threw myself forward, rolling awkwardly. I had no idea where the ball went. I ended up on all fours, facing the wrong way, feeling stupid.

I stood up to face the music.

All the Keeper said was, 'Goal.'

I looked behind me and saw that the ball had come to a stop exactly where an intelligent striker would be. Yes, goal. No doubt about it.

'Let me try again,' I said.

The same thing happened. I couldn't understand it. It was such a simple thing. Just a turn in the air. So why did I get it so hopelessly wrong?

'Because you still have to *think* about it,' the Keeper said. 'You still have to *picture* what your body must do. There is no time for that. There is no time for your head to send messages to the rest of your body and for your body to turn these messages into actions. It must be automatic. It must be *instinct*.'

I was discouraged. 'I don't think I have this instinct,' I said miserably.

The Keeper's reaction to this was so quick and fierce and out of character that I think my mouth fell open.

'Do not say that. Never say that! Are you telling me after all this time that I was wrong about you? I am not wrong about you. I *cannot* be wrong about you. If I am wrong about you we are all … *stuck*.'

69

He turned away from me. His shape seemed to wobble, to look frail.

I thought, *All? Stuck?* What does he mean?

He turned back to me, and became more solid. He seemed to be keeping himself visible by sheer will power. I could see that he was struggling.

He steadied, and said, 'You have this instinct. I see it in you. It's just that you do not see it in yourself. It is because you think you are still that awkward boy who walked into this clearing long ago. You think you are still that boy, except that you have learnt things from me.'

He was right. Deep inside of me, still, that clumsy Cigüeña lived. All legs and struggling wings and shame. Laughed at.

'You are not that boy any longer,' the Keeper said. 'He has gone. You have become someone else.'

He turned away and walked towards the shadow wall of the forest. Before he disappeared he faced me and said, 'Tomorrow I will show you who you are now.'"

"ISTEPPED INTO the clearing and saw him straight away. He was standing, motionless, at the very edge of the sunlight, where it was broken into fragments by leaf shadow. When he stepped forward, my eyes played a strange trick: some of that complicated shadow seemed to come with him. A piece of that patchy yellowish shade became solid and slouched beside him as he moved. It rippled. It kept pace with the Keeper as he walked calmly down towards me. A light wind was blowing into my face that afternoon, and I smelt her at the same moment she turned her pale muzzle and cold yellow eyes towards me.

A jaguar.

I saw her beauty while I struggled not to wet myself from fear. I saw how she carried the broken light of the forest on her fur, the dark markings against the pale gold, and I saw that these markings gathered themselves into circles like the petals of black roses. Her shoulder blades almost met at the top of her back, sliding against each other as she paced. Her feet were huge, and she placed them on the turf with a lazy precision. Her pale narrow belly swung slightly as she walked. She carried her tail in a stiff curve just above the grass.

The Keeper strolled beside her as calmly as a man walking his dog in a city park. But there was nothing tame about her. She was alert in this unfamiliar open space. Her eyes were fixed on me; her nose read whatever scents were on the wind.

The Keeper stopped fifteen metres from me, but the jaguar came on. She came towards me with the same slow loose stride, but I thought there was a tenseness in her now, a slight lowering of her body. The trembling that had begun in my legs took complete control of me.

'Don't move,' the Keeper said.

As if I could! As if my body would do what I told it to!

The great cat stalked past me, just a metre away. Then she turned and stopped where the breeze carried my scent to her. She lifted her head and narrowed her eyes. What she smelt, of course, was my fear, and this seemed to satisfy her. She sat. She was close enough to rip open my legs with one sweep of her claws. I had a mad desire to reach out to her and stroke her head, as if she were an ordinary cat, a domestic pet.

'Keep still,' the Keeper said, beginning to walk towards

me. The jaguar turned her head and watched him approach. Then she stood and ambled off to the shaded side of the clearing, where she lay down and began to wash the underside of her right foreleg with her tongue.

If the Keeper knew that he had terrified me, he gave no sign of it. 'She recognized you,' is all he said, looking at her, not me. Then he said, 'Come.' I was surprised to discover that I could walk. We moved to the edge of the clearing opposite the jaguar. I felt her yellow gaze on my back. When we stopped she returned to her grooming. The light seemed to be concentrated in her; she glowed, she burned. The silence was intense; I could hear the soft rasp of her tongue against her fur.

Then, suddenly, I saw her ears lift and twitch. She became absolutely still.

'Now,' the Keeper said softly.

From off to our right there came the slightest of sounds, a whisper of leaves moving against other leaves. Then a tiny disturbance in the undergrowth. I could just make out a pale shape, and then, concentrating, I saw the head and shoulders of some sort of animal. It moved, anxious and alert, into the clearing. I knew what it was, even though I had never seen one before. A small deer, not much bigger than a large dog, with a narrow, intelligent head, big ears, and a long slender neck. Uncle Feliciano called these deer 'little ghosts', partly because they were pale, partly because they were hardly ever seen. I had seen their droppings, like little black beans, but never the animals themselves. They were intensely shy and cautious. Some power greater than its own nature must have brought this one here, to where something terrible was waiting. It hurt my heart, knowing what was going to happen.

The jaguar had moved. She was now flat to the ground, facing the clearing. Her ears were down on her skull. Her great haunches were the highest part of her body, ready to propel her forward. The shadows of the leaves blended with her markings to make her almost invisible.

The deer was now clear of the trees. He moved, stopped, listened, moved again. His forelegs were very thin and delicate, although the knees were large knobs of bone. All his strength seemed to be gathered in his hind legs and haunches, which looked as though they belonged to a much larger animal. As I watched, his thin tongue slid out of his mouth and into his left, and then his right, nostril. Then he lifted his nose and tasted the air.

He was clearly nervous and confused to find himself in an open green space; such a thing was not part of his experience. He lowered his head to nibble at the turf, then lifted it again, quickly. He moved in little jerky paces further into the open. Then he seemed to hear something, and turned, head high and ears swivelling. His eyes were big, and moist as if with tears.

As soon as the deer turned, the jaguar came along the shadow-line, fast. She carried herself low to the ground, so low that I could not see her feet move beneath her. As soon as the deer moved again, the jaguar froze, blending into the dappled light beneath the trees. I glanced sideways at the Keeper. He too was watching this dance of death; but there was no expression in his shaded face.

It took about five minutes. Each time the anxious deer moved and turned, the jaguar rippled along the ground. And as soon as the deer lifted his head to smell the wind and search the shadows, she flattened herself and became invisible. I realized what she was doing: she was positioning herself so that the deer would eventually be caught between her and the goal. The goal and its net were the trap; that was where she would make the kill. But the cat had to time it very carefully, because the breeze would carry her scent to the deer at the very moment she reached her perfect position.

It happened suddenly. The deer was twenty-five metres from the goal, facing it, perhaps trying to puzzle out what this strange thing was. The jaguar came into the open behind him, belly touching the grass, tail snaking from side to side. She covered twenty metres, and then went into a crouch, her shoulders shoved forward. The huge muscles of her hind legs tensed for the spring; I could see them shifting beneath her skin. The deer had only to turn his head to see her, but the sharp fierce stink of the cat reached him first. He took off in a vertical leap, all four hooves clear of the ground, and spun round – all in one frantic movement. Before he touched the grass again the cat had completed her first enormous bound and her hind legs were swinging forward to launch her into the next. The deer twisted and leapt again, in high wild arcs towards the goalmouth. And then he seemed to understand what the net was, and that he had to escape it. He leant to change the direction of his next leap, but the jaguar was almost upon him now, and she had known that he would do this. She made her final spring. I could see clearly what was going to happen: the arc of the jaguar and the arc of the deer would meet; she would take him in mid-flight.

But then the deer did something incredible. He turned, in the air, onto his back and arched himself, switching the direction of his flight, and for just a fraction of a second he was clear of the cat and she was passing beneath him. What happened next took place in the flicker of an eye, but I saw it in dreamy slow motion. The jaguar seemed to hang in the air, as if gravity had stopped working on her. She rolled, and turned her head and shoulders back so that she was bent almost double. Her heavy right paw swung up at the deer. And she reached him, just. Her claws snagged and tore the muscle of the deer's hind leg. I saw blood in the air, droplets of blood like a string of red beads.

Then the laws of gravity and normal time were switched back on. The stricken deer fell, landing on his side, legs flailing. The jaguar landed on her feet two paces from her prey. There seemed no time at all between her landing and her going in for the kill; the actions flowed together.

I steeled myself to watch. I expected ripping and tearing, but it didn't happen. The jaguar pressed one heavy foreleg across the struggling deer and, almost gently, took his throat in her jaws and clamped them shut, closing his windpipe. She throttled him. When the wild jerking of his legs stopped, she released his throat and lowered herself onto the grass. She lay there, panting, for a minute, then walked cautiously around the corpse. Twice, she pulled and poked at it with a forepaw. Eventually, she took the deer's neck in her mouth and dragged the corpse beyond the ancient goalmouth into the darkness of the forest.

The Keeper did not speak, so after some moments I turned to look at him.

'So,' I said, 'what am I? The jaguar or the deer?'

It was meant to be a joke – the kind of joke seriously nervous people make. The Keeper gave no sign that he had heard me.

'Did you see what I wanted you to see?' he asked me.

'I think so,' I said. 'But I could not do what she did. I am human. It is not possible.'

The Keeper walked a few paces from me, faced me and said, 'Are you saying that it is *im*possible?'

I chose to say nothing.

He said, 'You are still very young. What do you know about what is possible or impossible? I tell you this: you will do things that now seem impossible. They seem impossible now only because you cannot imagine them. Because you do not believe in them. But you will do them, and afterwards you will be amazed that you ever doubted yourself. Now, let me ask *you* that question. Which are you? Are you the jaguar or the deer?'

'The jaguar,' I said. What else could I say?"

"I HAD MY fifteenth birthday two weeks before Easter, and when the holiday came I left school and did not go back. A week after the fiesta, while the little kids were still finding burnt-out rockets from the fireworks display, I climbed into the back of a pick-up truck with my father and other men and went to work. It was raining, and we all wrapped ourselves in black waterproof ponchos. The road was cut into deep ruts by the heavy tractors, and the truck slid and lurched. In the back, we constantly fell against each other and there was a great deal of cursing, which distressed my father because I was with him.

I asked him how long it would take us to get where we were going. I was ashamed of myself, realizing that I did not know even this basic detail of my father's daily life.

'In this weather,' he said, 'almost an hour.' From the way he said it, he seemed to expect me to be impressed.

In fact, I was dismayed.

'You know,' my father said, 'when I started logging, it took maybe fifteen minutes to get to where we were cutting. Every year it takes longer. It's amazing how much of the forest we have cleared.'

And as we travelled, the forest began to show its scars. On both sides of the road there appeared vast areas from which every tall tree had vanished. What grew instead was a thin green skin of scrub and creeper. Above these shaven landscapes the grey sky was suddenly huge.

Further on, the forest showed its open wounds. It had been scalped. Vast hillsides had been reduced to red mud and blackened stumps. Here and there low cliffs of rock poked through the soil like naked bone. I simply stared at all this, too dazed to speak.

We arrived at last at what Father called 'the camp'. The rain had stopped, but the air was still wet and heavy, and getting hot. Steam rose from the soaked earth and from puddles the colour of tea. I threw off the heavy poncho and jumped out of the truck to stretch my aching legs. I looked around and saw that I had been brought to a place where a terrible battle had been fought. Looking around at where I might spend the rest of my working life, I felt as though my heart were dying.

Our truck was one of many parked at the edge of an area of levelled gravel about the size of a big city plaza. Along one side of this space there were several metal sheds, blue or yellow, all blistered and streaked with rust. They had numbers painted on them, but the numbers were not in any particular order. Some of the sheds had great openings in their sides that could be closed with heavy roller blinds made of steel strips. Each shed like this had a huge workbench in front of it rigged up out of scaffolding poles, timber and sheets of steel. These benches had roofs made of filthy heavy plastic sheets bolted onto scaffolding.

On the workbenches were lumps of engine-guts, dismantled chainsaws, the broken arms of machinery. Already men were working at these benches, wrestling with screaming power drills that hung from chains, welding in storms of brilliant sparks, bent over lathes cooled by jets of dirty water.

On the opposite side of the camp stood a row of huge, damaged machines smeared with red mud. Many had terrible weapons attached to their snouts: thick gleaming spikes of steel, pairs of jaws fed by rubber hoses, scoop-shaped blades. Some had had wheels amputated. Their stumps were propped on wooden blocks, bleeding oil. They all looked like casualties of a disastrous war. Men in orange overalls climbed over and wriggled under these wounded machines, reaching into their innards. I remembered animal corpses I had seen in the forest, and the ants and maggots that were working on them.

Of the forest, here, there was no trace. No, that's not quite true: I was standing in its ruin. Beyond the camp, in every direction, there was a wasteland: stumps whose roots groped the air, shattered branches rotting in puddles of brown water, torn bark all over the place. The remains of fires smoked the air, which was dense with the stink of sour ashes and diesel oil.

My father and another man were unloading crates of bottled water and big plastic canisters of fuel from the back of the truck.

'Where are the trees, Father?' I asked him.

He looked round at me, smiling blankly. 'What trees?'

'The trees, Father. The forest. Where is it? Are we not there yet?'

'You mean where we are cutting? That way. About two kilometres.' He gestured.

I peered into the smoking distance and could just make out a low, dark ragged line between the grey haze and the grey sky.

My father looked at his watch. 'Ten minutes before I have to go,' he said. 'Come and meet your boss.'"

"My father had managed to get me a job in the tool shop. He was very pleased that he had done this because it showed that he was respected. Most boys, he said, had to start with the cutting crews. They began as what he called 'saw-monkeys'. Saw-monkeys had to dash from place to place carrying chainsaws that were still running, because the cutters lost time if they had to start up the saws in every new place. Saw-monkeys were always the first to be sent in to where a tree had fallen – and everyone knew that it was a good idea to wait for a while after a tree had fallen. That is because not everything that had lived on or near the tree vanished into the forest straight away. Snakes, in particular, were very stubborn, and would often hide close to the fallen tree. Many saw-monkeys were bitten by snakes.

Saw-monkeys had to carry heavy steel cables to the fallen tree and lock them on, so that the big dragging machines could tear the tree out of the forest. And if the cutting was on a slope, and if there had been rain, the logs were sometimes pulled down on top of the saw-monkeys and they would be crushed to death. Sometimes, not often, but sometimes, a cable would snap and whip back; in the past couple of years three saw-monkeys had been killed by broken cables. One had been cut in half at the waist like a piece of cheese sliced by a wire. The captain of that crew had told my father that the top half of the saw-monkey's body had landed on the ground while the bottom half was still standing on its legs.

So my father was pleased that he had wangled me a safe job at the camp. The pay was better, too.

The problem was, Paul," said El Gato, "that I was now, in my mind and in my heart and in my soul, a footballer. When my father first came home and told us that he had secured this job for me in the tool shop, he was very proud. My mother thanked God and hugged me. I am ashamed to say that I felt no gratitude, nor even any interest. And I know this hurt my father, although he did not show it. I did not even bother to ask him what the tool shop was. So on that first day, when he led me across the camp towards the drilling and the hammering and the workbenches, I had no idea what to expect.

My father led me to the door of one of the blue-painted metal sheds. We went inside and he took off his cap and knocked at a door to our left. No one answered. He knocked again, more loudly. We heard shouting approach the door. It was pulled open by a short, stocky man who was yelling into a two-way radiophone. He was completely, shiningly bald. He hardly looked at us, just jerked his head to tell us to enter. He stalked across to an open window and stuck the upper half of his body out of it, still yelling into the phone. Father and I stood awkwardly in the middle of the office, staring at the man's backside.

'How the hell am I supposed to do that?' The boss spoke with some foreign accent that made him sound angrier than he already was.

We could not hear the reply through the hiss and crackle that came from the phone.

'Of course it's impossible! Of course it is! I'm in the middle of a godforsaken jungle!'

More hiss and crackle.

'I don't care what he says! I want all of that stuff here in a week. All of it, do you hear me? And you can tell him that if it isn't, I'm gonna come up there with some of these crazy jungle guys and trash his stinking office!'

Hiss, crackle, squawk.

Amongst the papers on the boss's desk was an ashtray, and balanced on the lip of this ashtray was a burning cigarette with a long grey worm of ash. I noticed my father watching this cigarette, and I could see that it was making him nervous. As soon as that ash fell off, the burning stub would tip onto the mess of paper.

'Yah, tell him that I threatened him. You do that. You do just that, OK?'

My father darted forward, flipped the cigarette into the ashtray, then shot back to my side and stood perfectly still, like a child pretending that he had not done something naughty. I looked at him, but he would not meet my eye.

The boss pulled himself out of the window, cursing horribly, went to the desk, slammed down his phone, stubbed out the cigarette, and turned to face us. I was amazed to see the rage vanish from his face in an instant, to be replaced by a sweet smile.

'Good morning, gentlemen,' he said calmly.

'Señor Hellman,' my father said. 'This is my son, the one we have spoken about. He starts today.'

Hellman came across to me and ran his hand up my right arm, like a farmer checking the meat on an animal. He looked up at me; I was much taller than he was. I could have rested my chin on his smooth round head.

'He's a big one,' he said. 'What do you feed him on?'

'He is a good boy,' my father said. 'He is grateful to you for this work in the tool shop.'

'Yah,' Hellman said. He didn't sound as though he believed it. 'What can he do? Does he know welding? Electrics? Hydraulics?'

'He is a good learner, Señor Hellman. And very strong, as you see.'

'Yah,' Hellman said again. 'Can he write?'

'I can write,' I said.

'Good. Because the first thing you do is fill in this form.' He took a sheet of yellow paper from the desk and gave it to me. I think he was surprised that I did not move my lips when I read it.

A siren sounded from outside and my father twitched. 'Excuse me now, Señor Hellman,' he said. 'That is my call.' He turned to me, and clearly there were several things he wanted to say to me. But all he said was, 'I'll see you later. Listen to what Señor Hellman tells you.' Then he left.

Hellman pulled a metal chair to the desk and gave me a pen. The radiophone crackled and a voice like a robot's said something. Hellman picked it up, pressed a button and again thrust himself half out of the window and began shouting. I filled in the form and signed my name at the bottom. I felt that I had signed my own death warrant.

The boss was still hanging out of the window. I looked around the office and saw that the wall behind me was plastered in photographs of football players and football teams.

Hellman took me outside to a workbench and turned me over to a mechanic called Estevan. He was a small, very dark-skinned man, older than my father. He had a gold ring through the top part of his ear, and when he smiled – which was not often – he showed a gold front tooth. On his left hand there were just two fingers and a thumb.

Hellman told Estevan, 'This is your new boy. Let him watch what you do, OK? And answer his questions, no matter how stupid they are. Maybe give him some simple thing to do. His father says he's a good learner.'

Estevan looked at me, but spoke to Hellman. 'This is a giant,' he said. 'You should give him a job pulling up trees by hand. I tell you what. Get some more of these boy giants, and I won't have to spend so much time fixing these damn tractors.'

'Yah, yah,' Hellman said, almost smiling. He turned away towards the office, then turned back. 'Another thing, Estevan. Don't give this kid any of that cheap stinking brandy you think I don't know you got in your back pocket, OK? He would maybe like to keep both his hands.'

Yes, I thought. I would like to keep both my hands."

"It was a long day, that first day. It is hard to ask sensible questions about how a man does things when you have no idea what he is doing in the first place. Estevan was working on what he called a 'junction'. This was a plate of steel as long as my arm and as wide as my hand, studded with metal connectors and sprouting rubber hoses. I could not imagine what this thing was, but I didn't like the look of it.

As Hellman had done, Estevan felt my arm. He gave me a little glimpse of his gold tooth and told me to hold the ends of the steel plate. He then began unlocking the hose connections with a big adjustable spanner. The plate bucked as he wrenched at the nuts, but I put my elbows on the bench and held the thing steady. We took the whole thing to pieces. It took a long time.

'What are we doing?' I asked.

'It is cracked,' he said.

'What is?'

Estevan sighed dramatically, a man talking to a complete imbecile. He held the stripped-down plate in front of my face. There were ten holes in it where the hoses had been. Estevan ran his finger under three of the holes. I could just see a line, like a hair, running between them.

'Is it serious?' I asked.

He didn't answer. He just looked at me sorrowfully, the way you might look at a dog with three legs. Then he put the faulty plate under his arm and set off down the line of workbenches. I supposed I was meant to follow him, so I did.

The smith's bench was bigger than the others. Sheets

and bars of different metals were stacked behind it.

The smith was a big man whose face was all beard and spectacles. Estevan gave him the plate. He and the smith had a conversation which to me seemed like a violent argument, with lots of arm-waving; but it ended in smiles, with the bearded man's arm around Estevan's shoulders.

Estevan gestured to me in a secretive way, and I followed him round to the back of the metal sheds where the gravel ended and the mud and ruin of the forest began. He faced this wasteland and had a long pee into it. When he had finished he sighed with pleasure, pulled a flat bottle from his back pocket and took a swig. Then he squatted in the shade of the sheds and became as still as a waxwork statue. I did not know what else to do, so I did the same.

We sat there for an hour, I guess. I stared out at the vast expanse of water-filled craters and smouldering fires that had once been a forest. The only living things that still existed were the flies that were interested in my mouth and eyes. I wondered where everything else had gone. I suddenly realized that this was the hour of the day when I should have reported to the Keeper, and I felt a sickness, a guilt, a twist of misery in my guts. I imagined him standing in the clearing, looking around with his shadowed eyes, waiting for me. I put my forehead on my knees and tried to give up hope.

Estevan stood up; an alarm clock that nobody else could hear had gone off in his dark head. He stretched and looked around, and seemed slightly surprised to see me there.

'Come,' he said. 'Let's see if that hairy-faced so-called smith has cut our plate.'

The new steel plate – blank, with no holes, and no cracks – was waiting for us. We took it back to our bench along with the old one and spent the rest of the day drilling and building the new junction. Estevan worked with extreme care, and incredibly slowly. He said maybe ten words to me the whole time. I thought I would go crazy. I was deeply, deeply bored, and completely mystified. But for my father's sake I struggled to stay focused. Towards the end of the day Estevan made me use the big electric drill that was bolted to the roof of our bench. I did OK. Driving through the steel plate, the drill produced curls of metal. One touched my left hand and immediately drew blood. When this happened Estevan smiled and nodded as if he had revealed to me one of the secrets of the universe.

When the light began to drain from the sky Hellman came out of his office and went to the big grey generator at the far end of the work sheds. There was a change in the rhythm that came from the generator, and arc-lights came on all around the camp. The light was shocking. It took the colour out of everything. The surrounding emptiness took on a greater darkness; it was as if nothing but the camp existed in an endless space.

Because of the racket from the other workbenches and the growling of the generator I did not hear the tractors returning from the forest. So I was surprised to look up and see my father and Hellman watching me work. The light from the bright lamps bounced off Hellman's shiny head and lit up the wiry hair on my father's. My father's face was full of anxious questions, and hope, and a terrifying desire to be pleased.

Hellman said, 'So how was the boy, Estevan? You want to keep him? Or is he a saw-monkey?'

Estevan yanked on the big adjustable spanner and locked the last nut into place. I pretended not to care about what he was going to say, but I did, desperately.

'He will do. He is less useless than the last one. Leave him with me.'"

"On the long journey back in the truck I fell asleep with my head against my father's shoulder. He must have been very tired from his own work, but he sat upright the whole way so that I would not fall onto the floor of the truck."

"SO THE WEEK passed. Estevan taught me, almost word-lessly, to do things I did not want to do. Hellman watched, from time to time. I think he was pleased with me, but it was hard to tell. Towards the end of each day the harsh lights came on, and I would look up to see my father's face, watching anxiously. Then the long trip home to the meal my mother and grandmother had prepared. I ate ravenously while my family nudged each other and smiled. Then I went to sleep to dream tortured dreams of the Keeper, pacing the clearing, waiting.

On Saturday we all went to work as usual, but at midday a siren blew as the logging crews returned from the forest on their trucks and tractors and trailers. I went to stand in a line with Estevan and the other tool-shop men outside Hellman's metal shed. The Pay Man stood at a window above us and handed down a brown envelope to each of us in turn. Most of the men opened their envelopes as soon as they had them and counted the money inside. I did not, but then my father found me and encouraged me to open my pay packet and rejoice at the money.

I thought that once all this was done, we would go home. And some of the men did go, in a hurry to get back to town and give the money to their wives or to the girls who were already polishing the beer glasses at the café. But most of the men did not leave. Instead, they set back out in the direction of the cutting. I had not gone this way before, but my father put his arm around my shoulders and led me. We all zigzagged down a winding dirt path and into a sort of square pit which had been cleared of tree-stumps and other rubbish. The dirt floor of the pit had been levelled, and at each end a goal had been made out of scaffolding poles and netting. A soccer pitch had been marked out more or less accurately with lines of crumbled chalk. A number of men and boys were already kicking a couple of footballs about in this rough arena. Half of them wore scruffy green T-shirts; half of them wore scruffy orange ones. There wasn't much else in the way of kit. Many of the players wore cut-off denims as shorts; some wore socks, others didn't; some wore trainers while others still had their work-boots on. Just one or two men had proper football boots. I sat down with my father on the sloping side of the arena and he turned to greet and exchange friendly insults with other spectators.

There was going to be a game. I felt my blood wake up.

For quite a long time nothing much happened. The two teams, the Loggers, in the green shirts, and the Camp, in orange, seemed to have more or less eleven players each, and they continued to kick the two balls about in an aimless way. I recognized two of the Loggers, boys who had left school and started work at the same time as me. One was the tall boy who had kept goal at the church end of the plaza. The other was a boy called Jao. I knew him well. He was not big, he was not skilful, but he was fierce, and he was a dirty player. In the plaza games, his nickname was El Carnicero, the Butcher, and he liked it. I looked at him now. He had torn the arms off his T-shirt and cut the legs off a pair of jeans. He had heavy work-boots on his feet. The exposed parts of his body looked liked bunches of hard wire covered in skin. He had had his hair cut off, and his mean narrow head was covered in short bristles like a wire brush. A saw-monkey.

Then there grew a chorus of cheers and hoots and whistles from the crowd. A short stocky man dressed, amazingly, in immaculate referee's kit trotted down the slope of the arena. Watch on each wrist. Whistle on a red ribbon. Black shirt, black shorts with a white stripe, black socks taped just below the knee. Like a ref who had walked off the TV screen and into this crazy place. The sunlight bounced off his perfectly bald head. It was Hellman.

Hellman collected one of the two balls from the kick-about and with a blast from his whistle commanded the other ball to be kicked away. The Loggers' team got into a ragged formation and shaped up for kick-off, with the Butcher in the centre of the pitch, his foot on the ball. But the team from the Camp had a problem, it seemed, and they gathered around Hellman, gesturing and shouting and pointing at the empty goalmouth at their end. They didn't have a keeper.

I can only say that I went into automatic. I was not really aware of what I was doing. I got up and made my way down through the shouting crowd and onto the pitch as if I were walking through someone else's dream. The Camp team was still busy with Hellman, and didn't see me when I went and stood in the goalmouth. Then the crowd started yelling: 'Ref! Ref! Goalie! Goalie!'

Hellman and all the players turned to look at me. Jao, the Butcher, was the first to recognize me. He walked away from the ball until he was about twenty yards from me, stopped there and put his hands on his hips. 'Cigüeña?' he said. 'What are you doing there, idiot?'

It was a pretty good question.

Hellman ran up and sent Jao back to the centre. He looked at me and shrugged, as if to say, 'Well, it's your problem.' Then he ran, looking very professional, back to the middle of the pitch and blew his whistle to begin the game.

From the very first kick it was obvious that this was not going to be a normal game played by the normal rules.

Hellman blew up for technical fouls – he was very tough on offside, and in the first couple of minutes gave free kicks for handballs, even though the players had taken the ball on the front of the shoulder with their arms down by their sides. On the other hand, he let savage tackles go unpunished, and from my position in the goalmouth I saw two punches and a kick in the back of the leg; but Hellman let them go.

The Camp team seemed better than the Logger team, or maybe less exhausted, and for the first part of the game I had nothing much to do. I stood five paces from my line, trying to watch the game with the Keeper's eyes. I suppose I looked pretty calm, compared to the tall boy in the other goal. He scampered anxiously around the box, touching one of his posts and then the other, shouting, pointing. But inwardly I did not have the calm or the balance that I had learnt in the forest. This was because I saw that this was not so much a game as a battle between two tribes. It had no pattern. There was no way I could read it. When the Loggers got the ball and advanced on my goal, I could not read the play because they had no plan. Every player who got the ball wanted only to show off, to do some trick or other to beat one or two of the players from the Camp. And the crowd encouraged this, yelling applause as if they were at a bullfight, not a game of football.

Eventually, after our team had failed to score in a couple of ragged attacks, the Loggers broke free and came charging down the pitch. Four of their players against three of ours, all of them yelling for the ball at the same time. Jao, the Butcher, was one of them. He came pounding towards me down the centre of the pitch, his right elbow jabbing at the face of the defender who was tracking him. A couple of rough tackles sent the ball out onto the Loggers' left wing, off to the right of my goal. It was picked up by a pale-skinned, dark-haired guy, and he ran at my goal with his head down. Jao and two other Loggers were screaming for the ball to be crossed. But the man with the ball was easy, so very easy, to read. He had only one idea in his head. He wanted to score; he was not going to cross the ball. He was right-footed, and so I moved across the goal to my right, although I knew he would not get his shot on target. He dropped his left shoulder, just a bit too far, and I watched his right foot hit the ball in just the wrong place. I saw the track the ball was going to take, and did not bother to move. It went past my right post, a metre the wrong side of it. The crowd roared as if it had been a near miss.

Before I could fetch the ball, the Butcher stuck his sweating face up at mine. He showed me a grin full of yellow teeth.

'Hey, Cigüeña,' he said. 'You were beat, man. Didn't even move. You can't keep goal, man. Get off the pitch, you idiot. You gonna get hurt if you don't.'

Hellman was blowing his whistle like crazy and waving at me to take the goal kick. I got the ball and put it on the smeared line of chalk six yards out from my goal and looked up to see who was moving, and to where. One of my attackers was being quietly beaten up by two of the Loggers; one had gone way out to the left to keep out of trouble. The midfield was a mess. For a couple of seconds, I just stood. The crowd was whistling and howling.

Then I spotted the man who looked like he might know where to make a run. He was watching me, but darted his head around constantly, checking where the defence was. There was a clear path for him, if he could get around the big man who was behind him. The big man looked slow, and I thought my player could pass him. The route he needed to take was as clear to me as a floodlit road on a dark night. I made the kick and dropped the ball into that road. I put a little backspin on so that it wouldn't bounce too much. My player faked a move the wrong way then turned onto the ball, losing the defender completely. He took the ball well on the inside of his foot, and there was no one between him and the Loggers' goal. I expected him to miss, because of the choices. When there is no one to challenge you, apart from the keeper, you have so many choices, and they confuse you. But this man did not miss. Three defenders were closing in on him, but he took a moment to steady himself, and as the Loggers' goalie rushed out he slipped the ball into the corner of the net with the inside of his left foot.

The Camp workers' section of the crowd roared, and

performed a Mexican wave – not very well. The Loggers' supporters whistled and jeered, their goalkeeper began a furious rant at his defence, and the goalscorer almost disappeared under the congratulations of his team-mates. I was not at all surprised that no one recognized the part I had played in the goal. And I told myself I didn't care. Yet I was ridiculously pleased when, just as the game was about to restart, the scorer turned to look at me and raised both arms above his head and applauded me.

Until just before half-time, nothing much happened to trouble me. When it came to attacking, the Loggers now had only one idea, which was to get the ball to the Butcher. He had already split the lip of the man marking him, and his fierceness obviously scared my defenders, who were not keen to get close to him. So he had more space than he should have had. But when the ball was crossed to him, the Butcher was so busy shoving and hacking at the defenders that he forgot all about me. He believed I was no good anyway. So it was easy for me to cut out the high balls and the low crosses before they reached him, and this happened several times. Once, when the ball was aimed at him, he launched himself into the air almost horizontally, intending to volley the ball in a spectacular way. But because he had just that one thought in his head – he was already hearing the applause – he was watching only the ball, and had no interest in where I was. I stepped quickly out of the goal and took the ball out of the air. The Butcher lashed his foot at nothing and landed in the dirt, arms and legs every-where. The crowd was still laughing after I'd thrown the ball into midfield.

I had made an enemy, and it was probably at that moment that the Butcher decided to hurt me as badly as possible. He got his chance just before Hellman whistled for half-time. The Loggers were trying to attack down their right wing. One of their players got round my left back, and although the ball was probably going out of play the left back brought the player down with a brutal two-footed tackle. Hellman not only gave a free kick, he produced a red card. I was surprised when the left back simply walked off the pitch without even protesting. He just walked off into the storm of whistling and booing. You have to remember that I had no experience of referees. I was amazed that in this brutal battle Hellman could have such authority. But, of course, I had no experience of bosses, either.

I did my best to organize my players into a defensive wall. I remembered what the Keeper had taught me: that the purpose of a defensive wall is not to stop a shot, but to tempt the man taking the kick into trying the shot you want him to make. But my players did not understand this. Worse than that, they did not link their arms together, so the Butcher was able to shove and elbow his way into the wall. Obviously, he was going to break out of that wall and charge at me the moment the kick was taken.

In fact, the player who took the kick went for the direct

shot at my goal. He did a big performance about signalling to his other forwards, trying to bluff our defence into expecting a pass. But his eyes were full of lies, and when he ran up to the ball he shifted his weight for the shot. It wasn't a bad shot: low, past the wall, some bend on it. I saw the track he had set for the ball and threw myself to the left, leaving my legs trailing in case the ball struck one of my players and went on a different path. It didn't, and I got all the fingers of my left hand onto the ball and pushed it outside the post. It was not too difficult, and I had a split second to shift my eyes. I saw the Butcher almost on me, and I saw that he was watching me, not the ball, because I was his target. And I saw his boots lifted at my face, and I saw in his eyes the picture of the damage he wanted to do to me.

And that was the first moment I understood how deeply the Keeper's teaching had reached into me. I did not *remember* the jaguar. I did not have time to remember, or think about, the big cat. It was not a matter of me *imitating* her beautiful agility, the way she shifted herself in the middle of her leap. At that moment I *was* her. Like hers, my body knew what to do. So instead of simply falling to the ground once I had made the save, I twisted so that my hips and legs pulled my body past the post. I landed on my hands and knees, feeling the skin tear, but feeling no pain, in time to see the Butcher crash into the steel upright of the goal centimetres from my face. His right foot hit the upright, throwing his body sideways and forward so that his raised arm, his angry red face and his chest struck it at almost the same instant. The steel upright vibrated, and he hit the ground so brokenly that for a dreadful moment I thought he was dead.

Hellman appeared in the goalmouth, whistling frantically. At the edge of my vision I saw the spectators stand to get a better view of the disaster. Hellman knelt beside the Butcher and pulled the unconscious boy's eyelids back. A number of men came out of the crowd to help, or perhaps just to interfere. Hellman seemed satisfied that the Butcher would live, so he stood up and blew for half-time. The Butcher was carried off towards the camp, leaving a thin dark trail of blood in the pale red dust.

I got to my feet and found Hellman's face close to mine. He looked at me as if I were a particularly difficult piece of machinery.

'Interesting,' he said.

There was no real pause in the game for half-time. Some of the players took drinks of water from bottles held out to them by spectators, but I was not thirsty. The teams changed ends. After a great deal of fuss in the crowd, a man emerged to replace the Butcher. From the way he walked onto the pitch it was clear that he was not going to be a problem.

So we began again. One–nil.

Hellman had a tough time controlling the second half of

the battle. He followed the game very well, and was never far from the ball, but the crowd had more power than he had. Vicious tackles were applauded by the crowd, and so several times I saw Hellman put the whistle to his mouth to blow for a foul only to let play continue. Hellman was a strong man, but a crowd sometimes has more power over a game than the referee.

So, just as in the first half, the game was very wild and hard to read. Several times I had to clear desperate back-passes from my own players. Most of my saves had to be made among a whirl of legs and flying feet, and I had to curl and fold my body around the ball to protect myself.

Then Hellman gave a penalty. One of my defenders made a crazy tackle in the box, bringing down one of the Loggers from behind. There was no need for it, because the attacker was completely off balance and had no chance of scoring. But he was a good actor, and fell in a spectacular way, rolling over and over and finally lying face down in the dirt like a man who had been shot. The Loggers in the crowd let loose a storm of whistles and screams, and their players surrounded Hellman, waving their arms, falling to their knees and raising their eyes to heaven as if praying to the Holy Virgin. It was like watching a play in a madhouse. Hellman fought his way off to the left of my goal, still surrounded by protesting and appealing players. The ball had rolled gently to my feet, so I just picked it up and placed it on the penalty spot. I walked backwards halfway to the goal and stood waiting.

For whatever reason, doing that calmed everything. My own players turned to me and stared as if I had done something completely insane. One of the Loggers put both his hands on Hellman's shoulders and swivelled him round so that he could see what I had done. Hellman himself, who had been blowing on his whistle ferociously and trying to push players away from him, looked at me with a face that filled with surprise. The mob of players surrounding him parted, and he walked over to the ball and put his foot on it. He gave me a long hard look – but there was something in that look that was also kind. I had helped him out of trouble, and he knew it. He turned his back to me, and with his arms and his whistle drove everyone back behind the ball. I stayed exactly where I was, halfway between the ball and my goal-line.

One of the Loggers' defenders, a strong-looking black player, came up the field to take the kick. A huge wave of whistling came from the crowd. Hellman moved away from the ball and stood off to my right. I did not move back into the goalmouth. I was trying to fill myself with everything the Keeper had taught me about penalties. There was a mental battle to be fought between me and the penalty taker, and I was willing him to look at me, to look at me and see that he was more afraid of the situation than I was. Hellman blew a furious blast on his whistle and gestured to me to get back into the goal. And just as

I was going to move back, the Logger made the mistake of looking up and meeting my eyes. I saw that he was an intelligent man who understood what was going on. He tried very hard to tell me with his eyes that he was going to beat me, but I saw that really he was listening to the howling of the crowd and imagining, seeing, how terrible it would be for him to miss. So then I moved back onto my goal-line. He turned and walked seven paces back from the ball. I counted those paces and saw that he was going to shoot with his right foot. He stood still until Hellman blew the whistle. In those few tiny moments while he was waiting, I stood up straight and put my hands on my hips as if I were watching something that did not interest me much at all. I thought I was being very clever.

He took the shot exactly as I had expected him to. He did a good job of disguising it, but in the split second before he struck the ball he shifted his weight and told me that he was going to put the shot high to my right. I remembered that first day with the Keeper, him firing at me, me standing still, tears in my eyes, yelling 'Low, right!' or 'Left, high!' And, just as then, I knew where the shot was headed. So I launched myself into the path of the ball, arms flexed for the impact, hands wide open, my body facing out to the ball, my legs spread in the air. I was absolutely certain that some part of me – hands, arms, face, chest, thighs, legs, feet – would block the shot. In my mind I could see all the angles that the ball might follow.

What I had not thought of was the possibility that the kick would go wrong. I had not thought of that at all. Perhaps because he was nervous, he scuffed the shot. His foot scraped the ground at the same moment that it struck the ball, and the ball did not go where I was going. Instead, it wobbled towards the centre of the goal and the spot where I had been standing a split second earlier.

The scuff slowed the ball just a little bit, and that gave me the tiniest chance. I screwed my body round and threw my left hand into the ball's path, and my clawing fingers somehow got to it and tipped it over the bar. That hanging moment seemed to last for ever, and then time speeded up and I crashed to the ground on my back and shoulders. The impact slammed the breath out of me, and it felt as if I had broken every bone in my body. The world went brilliantly red and then completely dark for some moments. Then I felt myself being dragged to my feet and I was amidst my players, held up, kissed, shouted at, baffled. I got free of them and clutched the goalpost, fighting to get my breathing back and bring the pain to an end. Hanging onto that post, I lifted my head and saw – or imagined – a silver-black figure like a photo negative standing behind the goal, watching me. Then it disappeared, and I straightened up and turned round and found Hellman looking closely at my face.

'You are OK, yah?' he said. 'You want to go on?'

I nodded, managed to say, 'I'm OK.'

Hellman said, 'It's a corner. Are you ready for it?'

I nodded again. Hellman ran backwards, briskly, and whistled for the kick.

My defenders and the Loggers were pulling at each other, trying to find the space to block or shoot. The ball came in from the corner, too high for me and too far from me to take even if I had been feeling good. I was trying hard to concentrate on the movement of the ball, but the edges of my eyes were fuzzy. The corner didn't reach anyone in the Loggers' attack, and one of my defenders headed the ball out towards the midfield. It landed beautifully for one of the opposing players, who leant forward and took it down with his chest. He took it past two of the Camp players and when he was twenty yards out he struck a perfect half-volley at my goal. It came fast and it had swerve on it. I stopped it by pure animal instinct. I was still too groggy from the fall to follow the flight of the ball, but I fell to my left, arms and legs spread. The ball hit the inside of my left arm, which took the pace out of the shot. The ball landed close to where I fell, and I rolled onto it and covered it with my body. I had an overwhelming desire to sleep right there, in the dust, with my arms around the ball and feet stabbing at my head.

Hellman's whistle forced me to my feet. I bounced the ball twice, trying to win myself enough time and strength to kick it forward. But I couldn't. So I threw it out to a free player on the right wing. It was a good enough throw. My player took it well and went past a couple of half-hearted challenges almost to the Loggers' goal-line. He made a good cross and the same player who had scored for us in the first half met the ball sweetly with his head and put it past their goalie, who was expecting him to miss it and had his weight on the wrong foot.

Five minutes later, Hellman blew the final whistle. We had won two goals to nothing. My players surrounded me, ruffling my hair and giving high-fives and the rest of it. One or two of the Loggers shook my hand, which surprised me. Their penalty taker, the strong black player, was one of them.

'You had a game, man,' he said.

'I'm sorry about the penalty,' I said stupidly.

He grinned. 'I thought you were beat. What you did was impossible, man. And I screwed up the kick. You know that?'

'Yes,' I said. 'You were going top right. I went for it too early.'

'You did OK,' he said.

I nodded, not knowing what to say. I was not used to praise. He grinned again and turned to walk away. Then he stopped and turned round.

'And I never saw you before,' he said. 'Where'd you come from?'

'Out of the trees,' I said. I was still a bit woozy.

I went over to where my father was. His friends were

talking to him about me, and he was shuffling his feet and looking embarrassed. He was in a difficult position. He wanted to be proud of me, but I had helped beat his team. He was smiling and shaking his head at the same time. In the end he said, 'Your knees are a mess. We'll have to get them cleaned up when we get home. Your mother will have a fit.'

We walked back up to the trucks. As we were passing the metal sheds, Hellman, still smart in his referee's kit, came to the door of his office.

'Hey, kid!'

We stopped, my father and I, and faced him. Father looked anxious, because Hellman was frowning.

Hellman said, 'You're pretty good for a big heavy kid. Where'd you learn to keep goal like that? You are one of them superstars who play in the plaza back in town, yah? What do they call you?'

'They call me Cigüeña, boss,' I said.

Hellman looked at me, hard and suspicious. 'Stork? Why the hell they call you that?'

I shrugged, not knowing what to say. Or because it was a long story.

'OK,' said Hellman. 'But I want to see you play next Saturday, yah?'

'I don't know,' I said.

My father hit me in the ribs with his elbow.

'Yes, sir,' I said."

"THE NEXT DAY, Sunday, after church and the big meal, I waited until my family settled into the siesta and then I went into the forest.

I stepped into the clearing and looked left to where I expected to see the Keeper. He was not there.

I looked right and there he was, six yards in front of the goalmouth. As if waiting for a penalty. With his hands on his hips, just as I had stood in yesterday's game. He looked so *arrogant*, so ridiculously sure of himself. Just as I had. The ball was on the penalty spot.

I realized that he was mocking me. Many times, the Keeper had made me confront my own failings – my clumsiness, my lack of faith. This was the first time he had made me feel shame. The feeling bored into me like the fat tip of Estevan's drill. It was still twisting into me when it was followed by something worse. The Keeper had made me what I was, and there were no limits to my gratitude. But I had never imagined that he might *follow* me. I hadn't wanted to leave him, but the possibility that I *couldn't*, that he might haunt me for ever, everywhere, was terrifying. Hateful.

I walked over and faced him. 'You were watching, weren't you?' I had to force the words out. 'You were there at the camp when I kept goal.'

His mouth moved beneath the deep-shadowed eyes. The words followed. 'Of course.'

It was so matter-of-fact, the way he said it. As if he was confirming some trivial fact that I should already have known. My fear and my rage were, clearly, of no interest to him. He turned his back on me and walked into the goal-mouth. Then he faced me again, crouching.

'What now?' I said at last. I could hear the bitterness in my own voice.

The Keeper pointed to the ball. 'Be the penalty taker.'

'You know I cannot beat you,' I said.

The Keeper stood up straight. 'I know no such thing.'

'I have never beaten you. You have always known what I am thinking.'

'Then think something I cannot imagine,' the Keeper said. 'Hide your thought from me.'

It was a ridiculous, impossible, stupid challenge. I hated him. I took four paces back from the spot, a small voice in my brain saying, *I hate you.* My strike on the ball: *I hate you!*

I drove the shot to my right and low. The Keeper's body seemed to want to go in two directions at once; his upper body went to the right but hesitated. His hips and legs and feet seemed to be thinking differently, and threw his balance to the left. He staggered, recovered, and was on his way to meet the ball with his left hand when it flew past him and into the net, but he was lost, and too late. He ended up on one knee, his left hand on the ground. I had beaten him.

He didn't look at me. He took the ball from the net, rolled it in his hands, bounced it twice, and then held it.

'A good penalty,' he said. 'You hid your thought well. I could not read it at all.'

I looked down at the grass as if I had seen something really interesting there.

'Enough for today, I think,' he said. 'Your family will want you home. It is getting dark.'

I looked at the sky. The sun was still well above the shoulders of the trees."

"On Monday morning we travelled to work under a blue sky. A long cloud of red dust followed the pick-up. At the camp my father patted me on the back and then left me. I walked over to the steel sheds. Estevan was already at the bench, squinting at a worksheet clipped to a board. He looked up when my shadow fell on him. And then he did a strange thing. He bowed, making a fancy sweep of his arm like a servant in a comedy.

'Good morning, El Gato,' he said. 'I hope you are well, Gato.'

I looked at him. I thought he was being sarcastic in some mysterious way. I thought that perhaps I had done something wrong, something I did not know about. Puzzled, I remained silent.

Estevan straightened up and looked at me with great concern. 'El Gato?' he said. 'Has some other cat got your tongue, Gato? Is there something wrong?'

'I am fine, Señor Estevan,' I said at last. 'What is this "El Gato" thing?'

Estevan opened his eyes wide, two brown and white targets. 'You don't know? This is what everyone is calling you now, after the game on Saturday. I thought I had just a boy learning tool shop. Now I hear I have a great goalie working with me. El Gato, the Cat. The people here are saying, "Estevan, look after this boy. Keep his hands away from the drills, the blades. Make sure he does not get hurt like the others. He is like the cat, the *gato!*" Also,' said Estevan, 'I was at the game. You were quite good.'

Throughout the morning and the whole day, men who came to our bench or just passed it made a big thing of calling me 'Gato'. And that is where the name came from. Not from the papers, Paul, nor from players, but from that hellish place. And since then I have had no other name.

My second week at the camp passed much as the first

one had. I worked at the bench with Estevan, except when the two of us were wrestling with the greasy hydraulic guts of one of the giant yellow machines. And the end of each day was the same also: the jolting ride back to the town, arriving as the last of the plaza players were giving up the square to the darkness; wolfing down the meal, falling asleep exhausted in my hot small bedroom.

On Saturday, after we had queued for our pay, Estevan presented me with something in a plastic shopping bag. I was standing with my father.

'Come on, then, son, open it.'

'What is this, Señor Estevan?' I asked.

Estevan shrugged, glinting his gold tooth at me. 'Take a look.'

Something soft, black, folded. I spread it, and it was a new sweatshirt. On the back was a big white 1. On the front, Estevan had used some kind of white paint to draw a crude little picture of a leaping jaguar. My very first piece of kit. I did not know what to say. My father and Estevan were grinning at me like two monkeys. Then I became aware of another person standing behind me. I turned; Hellman was there, already dressed in his perfect referee's strip.

'Just because you have been given the number 1, this does not mean you have earned it,' he said. 'Anyway, put it on. We have a game to play.'

*   *   *

When we got to the red dirt pitch there were already many men waiting to watch the game. I was confused and embarrassed when some of them applauded me as I walked to the goal in front of the Camp team's supporters.

I was trembling. Not because of the crowd and what they were expecting of me. I was trembling on account of the spectator I could not see, and what he thought of me wearing the number 1 shirt. I walked round the back of the goal pretending to check the net. Was there, by one of the supports, a tall space where the air was colder and somehow denser? Perhaps. Or maybe what caused the shiver to run through me was remembering our last meeting in the forest – the fear and hatred that had overcome me, and had brought the Keeper to his knees. That moment had changed everything. We had moved onto a different level, the Keeper and I. I did not know how, exactly. It was something that I could only feel, like a cold discomfort in my stomach. I wasn't even sure whether he was there at the goal with me as my friend or my enemy. All I could do, the only thing I could possibly do, was play well. And go back into the forest the next day.

I stood in the goalmouth while Hellman blew on his whistle and the teams got into some kind of shape.

Our team was not the same eleven players who had played in the last game, but our goalscorer was there. Jao the Butcher was not mended enough to be part of the Loggers' team. His place had been taken by an older man, a very tall man. The Loggers had decided that maybe I could be beaten in the air.

And that is how they tried to defeat me. A great many high crosses, some of them good, came in at me. Most of them were floated across by a short, bristle-headed player. He was right-footed, but played out on their left wing, which puzzled me, at first. Then I realized why he was there. He was good at fighting his way to the goal-line and putting in his cross with the outside of his right foot, so that the ball curved away from me as it came over. When this happened, I had only two choices. I could try to force my way through the bodies in front of me and take the ball in the air. Or wait on my line for whatever kind of shot found its way through the ruck of players. I did not like either option, and I still don't. You have little control over what happens. Once, I had to punch the ball clear of the tall man's head with my left hand, which is the worst and most desperate save a keeper like me can make. But I managed to stop every shot that was on target, including one which deflected off the thigh of one of my defenders, so that I had to switch my weight and direction at the last moment to shove it round the post. I also had to slide onto a terrible back-pass which was picked up by the good black player whose penalty I had stopped in the last game. But by half-time, the Loggers had the smell of defeat coming off them. They had started to think that they would not get the ball past me.

As we changed ends, our good striker – his name was Augustino – put his arm around my shoulders.

'Will we win this one, Gato?'

'I think so,' I said. 'They smell a little bit beaten.'

Augustino laughed. 'Listen,' he said. 'The way it has been for a long time is this. The Loggers nearly always win. They are tougher than us.' He shrugged. 'The men used to bet on the game, but they stopped betting because we nearly always lost. But today, everyone is betting again. And we are favourites to win.'

'I think we will win,' I said.

'Because of you,' Augustino said.

'No. I do not score the goals.'

'My friend,' Augustino said, 'it is easy to score goals against a side who think they have already lost the game. And these guys think they have lost the game. And that is because of you. Strikers get very tired when they work and work and do not score. The way they get the energy back is to score. You have taken all the energy out of them. Do you understand what I am saying?'

'Yes,' I said. 'Someone told me this already.'

'That person was telling you the truth,' Augustino said.

Hellman blew a long blast on his whistle. We got into our positions and started play again.

We won the game three goals to nothing. Augustino scored one of them. I did not disgrace Estevan's shirt. My father lost ten dollars, and joined in the applause as I walked off the pitch. But my father's pride was no longer enough. I needed the respect of someone much harder to please. Someone who wanted something from me; someone who was waiting. Waiting with the kind of patience that only the dead have, because they have so much time."

"He materialized from the tree-shadows in the same instant that I stepped into the clearing. Immediately he dropped the ball in front of him and ran it down to the goal-line and positioned it for a corner-kick. He had never seemed to be in a hurry before, and I was surprised. Almost impatiently he signalled to me to get into the goal, and when I got there he sent over a high, in-swinging cross which I caught near the top-left corner. He gestured to me – again, that puzzling, hurried manner – and this time sent in a cross which cut back away from me. I couldn't get to it. Again a gesture, another corner. And another, and another. He had found a weakness in me. Well, not a weakness, exactly. He was reminding me that there is a kind of cross which keepers will always fear – the kind I'd had trouble with in the previous day's game at the camp. He began to send in ball after ball which came straight across and then swerved away from me towards the edge of the penalty area. In the clearing that afternoon, I dealt with most of them easily enough, coming fast out of goal and pulling them to my chest or else punching them away.

But it was too easy. We both knew it. He brought the ball

over to me and stood facing me.

'Tell me,' he said.

'I would not be able to do that in a game,' I said. 'I would be blocked in. Even if I screamed for the ball and my defenders let me out. Because the attackers would just stand there and let me run into them: no foul. Like yesterday.'

'Yes,' the Keeper said. 'So?'

'I don't know. Perhaps there is nothing you can do.'

The Keeper became agitated. It was very strange. His shape twitched and became slightly blurred at the edges, as if he wanted to be both here and somewhere else at the same time. This startled me. I was used to him being calm, expert, powerful. He dropped the ball and put his foot on top of it. Then he bent and picked it up. He turned away from me and faced the dark forest wall. He said something I couldn't quite hear.

'What?'

He turned back to me. 'How can I show you?' he said, and there was something very troubled in his shadowy voice. 'There is so little time.'

For the first time in two years he did not seem in control of me, or the space in the forest. Or himself. I felt sorry for him. I was amazed to feel that way. What are the words for what I had felt about him up to that moment? Terror, at first; fear, trust, respect, shame. Love, almost. Hate, sometimes. All big, big feelings. Now I had this small, cheap feeling – of being sorry for him. I was shocked to feel this way. And in that same moment I realized that I was now as tall as he was, and could do many of the things that he could do. I was growing out of him, like a child grows out of games and daydreams. It was not a feeling I liked. So I tried to make a joke.

'We need more players,' I said. 'We need a defensive wall for me to run against, attackers to face me. Perhaps you could call other players out of the trees.'

He looked at me as if this were a real possibility, as if he were considering doing something that was within his power, but which also terrified him.

The stupid smile I was wearing froze on my face.

'I was joking,' I said.

He looked at me as if I had spoken words in a foreign language. Then his face came back into focus; the shaky edges of his outline steadied.

'We do not have much time left,' he said.

I felt disturbed, hearing this a second time.

'Why not? What is going to happen?' I asked him. 'Are you going somewhere?'

'No, you are,' he said. He started to walk away from me, back towards that dark cloak of jungle.

'Please,' was all I could say.

He stopped, but did not turn round.

'Please,' I said again.

He turned and came back. I thought he would throw the

ball and resume our training, but he didn't. He stood two metres from me and said, 'Listen to me. Life changes. Change is everything – change is life itself. The only thing that stays the same is being dead, believe me. You have changed, and that is how life sings in you. When you first came here, you were weak and lonely and didn't know what you had within yourself. Now you know. You are a keeper. You know what you can do. Go out and do it.'

It sounded like a goodbye, a dismissal, and I wasn't ready. So I found something to say, something to keep him there with me.

'I still don't know what to do about that out-swinging corner,' I said.

'Stand on your line,' he replied. 'Stand on your line and expect the unexpected.'

I smiled. 'Another of your riddles.'

'No. The unexpected is the only thing you can depend on. This is what I have to tell you. The game always changes. If you are a player, you must change with it. Football, the kind of football I played, has gone. The power of the game moves. Now, midfield players score impossible free kicks from the halfway line. Fullbacks play like wingers. Centre-forwards play with their backs to the goal and lay the ball off to defenders coming through to strike. Everything is fluid. Everything is possible. Everything will change. You, especially. And you are lucky, in one way. You have a place to be, and a place to defend. The forest has taught you this. It is quite simple, after all. Like the forest, you will come up against teams who can think of only one thing: how to cut you down. Or how to get past you, around you, through you. And all you have to do is stop them. Which is something you can do now, because I have taught you how. You have something to defend, to protect. It is only a football goal, of course: three pieces of wood and a net. But this is more than most people have. And if you can protect that, then perhaps other things, more important things, can also be protected. Do you know what I am saying?'

Well, no, I did not know what he meant. I was, after all, very young. I felt as though a man much stronger than me was handing me a great burden because he could no longer carry it himself. It was not what I wanted. But I could think of nothing to say.

The Keeper turned towards the trees and walked away.

'Wait!' I called out to him, and he stopped and faced me. 'You said that I was going somewhere else. What did you mean? Where am I going?'

'I cannot tell you,' he said. 'I am not hiding anything from you. I do not know.'

We stared at each other across the clearing. I was almost as afraid as I had been the very first time we had stood there, so long ago. Then he turned away and melted into the gathering darkness of the forest."

PAUL FAUSTINO HAD interviewed hundreds of players, and trying to get them to describe the experience of playing, of winning or losing, a major game was almost always like trying to squeeze milk from a rock. Clichés dripped from these men with their sweat. But Gato was a different kind of animal altogether. He had described brutish kick-and-rush games in a logging camp in the middle of nowhere, and Faustino had found himself completely absorbed. He was desperate to get Gato to speak about the World Cup final in the same way that he had described those rough kick-abouts. The problem was that Gato had a different agenda. For whatever reason, he had chosen this interview to unload this wild fantasy about himself and the Keeper.

Faustino told himself to be patient. Midnight had come and gone, but he had to be patient. He squinted at the digital counter on the tape recorder. Plenty left.

The goalkeeper was speaking again.

"The next week, at the camp, Estevan was comically proud of me, calling passing workers over and introducing me: 'Hey, you know my boy, El Gato? Best player ever to come out of this stinking jungle. Hey, hey! Wipe your greasy hand before you shake his, man!'

On Thursday morning, the sky had a weird greenish tinge to it. As we lurched our way to work in the back of the pick-up, hard gusts of wind began to blow needles of rain into our faces. By the middle of the morning, the storm had burst upon the camp. The wind screeched through the gaps between the metal sheds, hurling and twisting sheets of rain among the workbenches and the hulking yellow machines. Most of the men switched off their machines and crowded into the storage sheds to smoke and wait. But Estevan was as stubborn as a mule, and insisted that we work on beneath the wild light of the bare bulbs that swung above our bench.

The storm drove the loggers out of the forest, and they came up to the camp. My father came across to us, his poncho slimed with red mud. He was clearly pleased that his son was one of the few still at work.

'Dear God,' he said, lifting his voice above the rage of the rain on the plastic roof. 'It's terrible down there. We almost lost a tractor, one of the big ones. It started to slide and the driver jumped. I don't blame him.'

Estevan sucked his teeth and shook his head, agreeing with my father while not troubling to interrupt his work with talk.

My father said, 'Every day I thank God that my son is not doing that work. You are still pleased with him, Estevan? You think he has a future?'

The old man lifted his head and looked across at me. He showed all of his gold tooth.

'This boy Gato? Oh yes. He has a future, I think, yes indeed. I think he will be very good one day, your son.'

I looked at my father. He was smiling, but his puzzled eyes moved from Estevan to me and back to Estevan again.

Before the end of the day the storm raged away to some other place. The sun returned to burn through the wet air, baking a thin crust onto the mud around us.

On Saturday, as we were queuing for our pay, three vehicles pulled into the camp. Two were the high-wheeled three-ton trucks that carried men over rough country to far logging sites. 'Sludge buses' is what Estevan called them. These were not from our camp, though, and the forty or so men who climbed down from them were strangers, although many of them wore the same bright green jerkins that our loggers wore. Estevan sent a boy across the compound to find out about them. The boy came back, excited. 'They are from Rio Salado, the camp at Salty River,' he said. 'They say they have come for the game.'

The third vehicle was a big black Mercedes-Benz four-wheel drive with those blue-tinted windows you can't see through from the outside. Its gleaming panels were clouded with dirt. It parked a little way from the sludge buses, and for a whole minute no one got out of it. Then the passenger door opened and a man stepped out and stretched. He could not have looked more out of place if he had landed from the moon. He had expensive dark hair and a grey moustache. His jacket, it seemed to me, was woven out of light; pale grey rippled into silver as he moved. Beneath the jacket he wore a silky black polo-neck sweater and his black trousers were tucked into calf-height brown leather boots. He looked like a rich tourist who had decided to go somewhere dirty for a change.

While I – and scores of other men – was gazing at this magical creature, Hellman's door banged open, and the boss came down the rough steps. He bustled across to the Mercedes and shook hands warmly with the elegant stranger; as he did so, the driver's door opened and a woman stepped out. A woman! There, in that place! The whole compound fell silent. She too was dressed as if going on holiday; but her holiday was going to be in a toy jungle. She was dressed like one of those old-time Hollywood actresses playing a part in a Tarzan movie: a tight-fitting safari suit the colour of milky coffee, lace-up boots, a dinky little rucksack over one shoulder. Her face was half hidden by big, purple-tinted sunglasses and a cloud of red-gold hair. She walked carefully round the front of the car and also shook hands with Hellman. Then Hellman walked his guests to his office, stood aside as they went in ahead of him, went in himself, and closed the door.

The compound exploded with noise. Men gave up their places in the pay queue to greet or insult or joke with the loggers from Rio Salado. Everyone had some comment to make about Hellman's mystery guests. The Pay Man was yelling madly, trying to get the men back into line. Something odd was happening, and I had a worrying feeling that it had something to do with me. Maybe not, though. After all, Hellman had walked the two visitors straight past me, not even glancing at me. I tried to clear my head – I had a game to play, a goal to protect, a ghost to impress. I went to the Pay Man's window, took my pay, found my father, gave the money to him. Then we walked with the crowd who were heading for the pitch.

The teams warmed up. We waited longer than usual for Hellman, but he came at last. The glamorous visitors were with him, and Hellman carried a rolled-up rug. Towards the bottom of the slope that led onto the rough pitch, he stopped and made a row of men shuffle closer together to make room for the rug, politely gesturing to the couple from the Mercedes. They sat down and looked around attentively. Hellman marched onto the pitch, blew, raised his right arm. The teams took up position. The practice balls were kicked away.

And that's when the trouble started. Augustino was the captain of our side that afternoon and was standing at the centre spot with his foot on the ball, waiting for Hellman to signal the start of the game. But before that could happen, Hellman was distracted by some sort of problem in the crowd. The men from Rio Salado had all sat together in the same place, of course; but now our supporters, the men from the camp, were yelling and screaming at them and making wild gestures towards the pitch. The Rio Salado men were laughing, making 'sit down' gestures back. The Loggers' supporters were doing the same thing. A few drinks cans were thrown. Hellman ran across to the troubled area of the crowd. At the same time, a number of our players gathered around Augustino.

By now, I had walked out of the goal to stand beside one of my defenders.

'What's going on?'

'I don't know,' he said. 'Something to do with that guy, there. You see him? The white guy, standing on the centre circle?'

I saw him. He was pale-skinned and fair-haired. He looked European. German, maybe, and old, for a player. At least thirty. He must have known that the fuss, the hold-up, was all about him; but he appeared quite unconcerned. He ran on the spot, he stretched, he put his hand on his left foot and then his right. And all the time he kept his eyes fixed on me.

I put my hand on my defender's shoulder. 'Do me a favour,' I said. 'Go up there and find out what's going on.'

I watched him run up the pitch and get lost in the mass of players from both sides who had now surrounded Hellman. Within thirty seconds, Hellman's whistle was screeching, and the knot of bodies around him reluctantly untied itself. Now I could see Hellman; he was making two-arm gestures to both teams: settle down, let's play the game, shut up. I looked across at where the elegant strangers were sitting on their rug. They looked completely relaxed about what was going on, as if it was exactly what they had expected. The woman was writing in a small notebook. The man had taken off his gleaming jacket, folded it neatly and placed it beside him. He too was looking closely at me.

My defender jogged back.

'Well?'

'That pale guy,' he said. 'He's what it's all about. He's from the Rio Salado camp. The Loggers brought him in. Augustino and the others are playing hell because he's not from here. Hellman says it doesn't matter, he's a logger, and one logger is the same as another.'

'So who is he?' I said, watching the strange player watching me.

My defender shrugged. 'They are calling him El Ladron,' he said. 'The Thief.'"

E L GATO LOOKED up at Faustino. "Mean anything to you?" he said. "El Ladron? The Thief?"

Paul Faustino put his hands behind his head and gazed at the ceiling. He liked this sort of thing, the testing of useless knowledge. He was seriously addicted to trivia quiz shows on TV.

"Let me see," he said. "I can think of three players called 'Ladron'. One of them was Spanish. Played for Real, I think. Then there is that Roberto Something-Something, the Mexican."

"That's two," El Gato said. "You said three."

"Yeah. The other one came from Sweden originally. Or his parents did." Faustino tapped his forefinger rapidly against the side of his head, as if his memory could be jogged from the outside. Which it could, apparently, because with a click of his fingers he said, "Larsson. That was it. He played here, years ago, for Sporting Club. An old-fashioned centre-forward, tough. A goal-poacher. I never saw him play, though. He was tipped for the national side, I seem to remember. Then something happened, and he vanished from the scene. An injury, was it?"

"Not to himself, Paul," said Gato. "He half killed a goalie in a Cup game, and after that he lost his nerve and no one would touch him. He was transferred to some Junior League club up north."

"And it was Larsson, this mystery player at the camp? What the hell was he doing there?"

Gato smiled. "Apparently, he'd quit professional football and joined the logging company his father worked for. He'd ended up at the Rio Salado camp. He was their star player. And our loggers had brought him in to deal with me, to take me out of the game. That's what we all thought, anyway. That was what our supporters thought, for sure. That's why they were going crazy. And that's why Augustino ran twenty yards back towards me and pointed to his eyes with one hand and to Larsson with the other. He was saying, 'Watch that guy; he's out to get you!'

But if the crowd was expecting fireworks, it didn't get them. Not at first. In the first half, our attackers seemed hypnotized, forever drifting back into our own half. They were expecting the battle to be fought between El Ladron and myself, and were behaving like spectators. Augustino was going crazy at them – every time he won the ball, he had to hold it up to wait for support.

And so the Loggers were able to run the game. I had to work much harder than in the earlier games. And, yes, Larsson made life very difficult for me. He was a short-range player, you know? Very quick over short distances – ten, fifteen yards. And he never seemed further away from me than that. He deserved his nickname – he was there to make confusion and then steal goals from half-chances. And he never avoided tackles. He just went through them somehow, as if he was doing the tackling, not being tackled. He was always onto me, always between me and the ball, so that I had to get round him or above him. If I got down to a low shot, I would look up and see his feet close to my face. When the Loggers won corners, Larsson would not look for a space in which to receive the ball. Instead, he came in close amongst my defenders, messing up their marking and their concentration. He was constantly shoved, pulled at, body-checked; but he never went down, never retaliated. It was as if he didn't even notice. He was there to crowd me, to rattle me, and nothing else mattered to him. He was the first professional I had played against, and I struggled to deal with him.

So I had to do a different kind of goalkeeping. With all the play in my own half, under attack all the time, there was not much point in trying to read the game or launch counter-attacks. I had to make a crazy number of reflex saves from close-range efforts by Larsson, as well as from some wild deflections and slices. I seemed to be on the ground for most of the first forty-five minutes. When I wasn't, I was twitching in the goalmouth like a spider when rain strikes its web. Also, I was scared. The feeling among the supporters and the players had got to me: I was waiting for El Ladron to damage me.

In fact, he was standing over me when Hellman blew half-time, and I was lying in the dirt hugging the ball, trying to make myself as small as possible. Then Larsson pulled on my arm to help me to my feet, and I found myself face to face with him. To my surprise, he winked at me; and then he turned away and jogged off to join the rest of his team at the centre spot. I realized something: Larsson hadn't given away a single free kick. He'd been in my face the whole time, but he hadn't actually fouled me once. What was going on? Was he biding his time? Were his instructions to cut me down during the second half? Was that what his wink was telling me?

'You did nothing to prepare me for this,' I said aloud. If I expected a reply from the Keeper, I didn't get one.

Augustino burned the team's ears at half-time, and we played with much more spirit in the second period. Larsson didn't see much of the ball for the first fifteen minutes or so, but was always making little runs, challenging defenders, chasing the ball, running at me. He had a lot of energy for an old man. Then Hellman gave a free kick to the Loggers just outside the box, about twenty yards out and just to my right. I screamed at my defenders and managed to get them into a wall in the right place. But they didn't link arms, and I watched helplessly as Larsson stole round the back of the wall and pushed his way into it from behind. The defender on the end of the wall was shoved sideways, blocking my view of the kick taker just as he shot. My best guess was that when the ball came round the wall it would be heading for the top-left corner of my goal, and I launched myself sideways into the air. I'd guessed right; but one of my backs made a heroic attempt to head the ball away. It struck him on the side of his face and ricocheted off course back towards my right. I was beaten, really, but somehow managed to hang in the air long enough to fling my right arm out and palm the ball over the bar with a desperate scooping movement. I crashed heavily down onto the hard earth, not sure if the roaring I could hear was coming from the crowd or from the inside of my own head. Someone helped me up. It was Larsson. He looked closely at me, smiling slightly, and tipped his pale head to one side as if to ask if I was OK. And that gesture changed the way I felt about him. He wasn't there to hurt me; he wasn't a hired assassin. He was all right.

I'd been conned. That caring gesture was just a tactic to put me off my guard, and for the last quarter of the game El Ladron hassled and jostled me, shoved me, grabbed my shirt, leant into me; and his face was as blank as a whitewashed wall. I lost the thread of the game; I was aware of him and only him: where he was, what he was going to do next. I was beginning to lose control of my goalmouth, too, because all I could do was focus on Larsson, on how to avoid him, how to defeat him.

A cross came in from my left, and it would have been an easy one for me to cut out. Except that Larsson stood on my foot as soon as I began to move out to it, and I fell on my face in the dirt. Hellman didn't blow for the foul. The ball went harmlessly out of play. I got to my feet and a main fuse went bang in my brain. I screamed at Hellman, but he simply ran backwards away up the pitch, signalling me to shut up and take the goal kick. I turned on Larsson, stalked towards him where he stood on the edge of the area. My fists were clenched, and it was as if a red fog closed in around everything except his bland, expressionless, punchable face.

Then the Keeper spoke to me. A clear, calm voice from somewhere behind me spoke straight into my skull. I can't remember the words he spoke. Perhaps he didn't use words. But his voice, and his presence, damped down the fire in me and blew the fog from my vision. It was as if a cooler blood filled my veins.

I stopped, turned. I was certain that I would see him there behind the net, shadow-faced, arms folded, invisible. But all I saw was a grinning logger who had come out of the crowd and put the ball down for the goal kick. There was now an enormous noise coming from the spectators, a noise like a wave that threatened to pile down on me and crush me. I walked back to the goal-line and held onto the post for a second, steadying my breathing. The anger that had filled me became something small and hot and red; something I could pluck out and throw away. I ran onto the ball and drove it upfield: a long, long kick that carried my fury away with it. I felt a wonderful coolness and calm wash over me. I had won. I was back in control. Larsson could not get to me.

Except that he did. Got to me and got past me, and in the last minutes of the game. After he'd brought me down he stayed outside my area, hardly bothering to run, not trying to lose his markers. He looked tired to me, and once or twice he bent over with his hands on his knees as if he was short of breath. Then he wandered away from the centre out onto the Loggers' right wing, as if declaring that he had nothing more to add to the game. So I relaxed, and that was stupid. When one of the Loggers lashed in a clumsy cross from their left wing, a cross that went over the heads of their attackers and bounced towards my arms, I took a leisurely pace towards the ball and waited for it. That's when Larsson, the Thief, came out of nowhere and earned his nickname. He arrived at great speed from my left, went past my amazed left back, who was watching the ball, leapt into its path with his arms high in the air, took it on his chest and turned it into the bottom-right corner of my goal. A goal worthy of the great Diego Maradona himself

– a goal made of nothing. I put my hands over my face; then, as a roar like the ocean washed around me, I put them over my ears.

On the ride home, my father kept his arm around my shoulders. He and the other men spoke at length about the great save I had made from the deflected free kick. It meant little to me. I had tasted defeat for the first time, and it was sour."

"LATER, I SAT with my father and my sister at the table outside the front of the house while my mother and grandmother cooked the Saturday evening dinner. The smell of chicken boiled with sweet peppers and chilli drifted out into the dusk. My sister was weaving her doll's hair into ridiculous styles; my father was reading the weekly newspaper and drinking beer. I played the afternoon's game over in my head while I watched a fat full moon rise over the trees. From the forest frogs were calling, trilling like a thousand distant telephones. We all looked up when we heard the sound of a car; traffic on the road was unusual at this time. We saw the lights as they passed the end of our track; then the brake lights flared and the engine paused. We heard the vehicle reversing, turning. The pepper tree and the corner of the house were bathed in light for a moment and then returned to darkness. The scrunch of tyres on gravel. Doors slamming.

My father got up and walked round the corner of the house to investigate. Almost at once he reappeared. He was holding his hands out in front of him, and they were making frantic little 'get up!' gestures. His eyes were swivelling like a frightened pony's. It was as if he had become some sort of mad person just by walking round the corner. I stood up and was amazed to see that the next person to appear was the movie star woman, now wearing a shining leather jacket over her jungle costume. Then the elegant man with the moustache. Then Hellman, dressed in smart jeans and a sweater. I did not recognize the fourth person at first. He looked a little like a monk, in a big loose grey sweatshirt with a hood. But as he came into the light he pulled this hood away from his face, which was pale, grey-eyed, smiling. It was Larsson. I just froze, my mouth hanging open. I must have looked like the village idiot.

My father dashed into the house, which was awkward for me because I had to pull myself together and ask the visitors to sit down. My sister stuck her finger in her mouth and gazed at these people from planet television.

I managed to say, 'You are welcome, and your guests, to our house, Señor Hellman.'

Hellman smiled and said, 'Thank you, Gato.'

It was the first time he had called me that. What the hell was going on?

My father returned with a tray carrying four glasses and a bottle of the cordial we only ever drank at Christmas.

He poured a little into the glasses and handed them to the guests. The glamorous woman asked for water instead. My father made a fancy gesture of apology and went back into the house. Another awkward silence. The man with the moustache sipped some of the cordial. My father reappeared with a glass of water and set it down in front of the woman. Then he sat down. At the same instant, all four guests stood up because my mother had come out of the house. The whole situation was getting ridiculous: up and down, up and down, and nobody saying anything. Mother sat down on a chair against the wall of the house. The guests sat down again and drank, or pretended to drink. Hellman said 'Cheers!' in English, then turned to my father and spoke with the greatest respect. He began by introducing his companions.

'Señor,' he said, 'allow me to introduce Señora da Silva. Her husband is Gilberto da Silva, the president of DSJ. This gentleman' – he gestured towards the man with the moustache – 'is Milton Acuna. He is director of football at DSJ.'

I knew – all the boys in the township knew – DSJ. Deportivo San Juan. Pictures of the team were splattered all over the walls of the café. We had roared at their victories, howled at their defeats. They were our local team. San Juan was only five hundred kilometres away. And, now that she was sitting opposite me, without the big sunglasses, I recognized Flora da Silva. Her husband owned DSJ but he had bought it with her money, and she ruled the roost. When DSJ were on TV it was always her the cameras lingered on as she sat in the directors' box. I was hypnotized."

"A good-looking woman," Faustino said, smiling. "I've been hypnotized by her once or twice myself."

El Gato smiled too. "I bet you have. But it wasn't her who had me sitting there starstruck. It was the great Milton Acuna. There were many fading photos of him on the café wall: a long-haired, dangerous-looking boy, in the pictures, more like an American rock star than a player. One of the best strikers ever to play for our country: fifty-eight goals in seventy-two matches, twenty years before. They had named an aftershave and a brand of clothing after him. And here he was, at our table, watching my face as I struggled to make sense of what was happening, and failed utterly.

Then Hellman looked at me and opened his hand towards Larsson. 'This man you know already. Today they called him El Ladron, and he did steal a goal from you. The Loggers did not ask him to play; I did. He played as a favour to me. I asked him to find out if you could be made to explode.'

Larsson reached across the table, put both his hands around one of mine and shook it. He looked into me with his pale European eyes and said, 'My friend here asked me to put you on a roller coaster, to make you feel down, up, down again. I was amazed at how cool you were. Also, you made one or two saves that I thought were impossible. I felt I had found the rage in you towards the end when I deliberately fouled you, but you somehow got yourself together. You are perhaps the best goalie I have played against. You do know why we are here, don't you?'

Señora da Silva spoke, addressing my father. 'We want to sign your son, Señor. Señor Hellman called Milton and said there was someone special we should come to see. We came. It was a long trip, but worth it. He is a keeper, your son. I have a contract in my bag. I also have a chequebook. When you sign the contract on behalf of your son, I will write a cheque for ten thousand dollars. The cheque will be made out to you, of course. Your son is not able to sign any legal agreement until he is eighteen, as I am sure you know.'

She took papers out of her expensive handbag and laid them on our poor table. 'The contract is for two years. If he proves to be unsuitable, the contract will end when the two years are over. However, we will pay him a salary of three hundred dollars a week for as long as he remains a member of DSJ. Very large match bonuses, should he play for the first team or the B team, are paid on top of that, of course. The terms of the contract allow us to sell him within that period. Ten per cent of any profit we make from such a sale will be paid into an account you specify. Do you have any questions you wish to ask me?'

The silence that followed this speech was intense. It seemed to me that even the frogs' chorus had ceased. As you can imagine, I simply could not believe what I had heard. I think I was in shock. Then, as the meaning of Señora da Silva's words sank in, I began to be filled with delight, with an outrageous joy. The Keeper has done it, I thought. He has rescued me. He has made this happen.

I did not dare look at my father's face. I was afraid of what I would see in it. Then someone spoke, and it took me a moment to realize that it was my mother.

'Forgive me, Señora,' she said, 'but you speak of my son like he is a thing, something you shop for in the market. It is not like that. My husband tells me that our son has a genius for football. I know nothing of this. In fact, I find it hard to believe. My son does not play football like the other boys. And he will not always work at the logging camp. He wants to be a scientist, perhaps a biologist, and we will help him. He loves the forest, and already knows a great deal about it. I hope you will pardon me, Señora, but as far as I am concerned, this football thing of yours has nothing to do with us.'

It was as if Señora da Silva had heard a statue speak. She stared uncomprehendingly at my mother for several moments. The muscles around her lips twitched. Then she turned to Hellman. The question in her face didn't need to be spoken.

Hellman looked uncomfortable. He said, 'The young man has spent a great deal of time deep in the trees that surround us here, Señora. At least, that is what his father has told me. I cannot explain how this has made him such a great keeper. As I said on the phone, there are things going on here that I do not understand.'

Señora da Silva shook her head as if it were surrounded by irritating flies. She spoke to my father, not my mother. 'I am a little confused,' she said. 'Señor Hellman told us that a boy had appeared from nowhere who was a born goalkeeper. Now I am told that he will be some kind of biologist.'

Now, at last, my father spoke.

'Please forgive my wife, Señora,' he said. 'She has ambitions for our son. A college education. Myself, I don't know. In a year or two, perhaps...' He trailed off. Maybe he felt my mother's eyes burning into the back of his neck. Then he struggled on. 'But my son shows promise as a mechanic. That is true, isn't it, Señor Hellman? A mechanic is a good thing to be, Señora. A real job. This football thing is, is...' He ran out of words.

Señora da Silva was clearly annoyed. 'To be frank, my husband is not especially interested in engineers or biologists, and nor am I. I did not drive all the way out here with Señor Acuna to meet someone who could fix my car or describe the mating habits of lizards.'

Another silence. A very uncomfortable one. I stared at the tabletop.

Señora da Silva leant back in her chair and tapped a polished fingernail on the papers in front of her. 'Is it the money? The terms are quite generous, considering that your son is only fifteen.' She shrugged. 'But there may be some room for negotiation.'

My father was dismayed that anyone should suggest that he could drive a hard bargain. 'No, no, Señora,' he said, hurriedly, 'it is not the money. The money is ... well...' His voice died on him again.

Señora da Silva glanced at Hellman. He would have told her what my father's wages were, of course. She would have worked out how many years it would take him to save ten thousand dollars.

Then Milton Acuna spoke for the first time.

'Señor,' he said, very calmly, 'this is all very *disturbing* for you, I am sure. Perhaps you and your wife would like a little time alone to discuss the issues.'

Señora da Silva flashed a glare at him. Acuna laid a calming hand on her wrist. My father turned to look at my mother. She nodded. My father got to his feet.

'A good idea,' he said. 'So if you will excuse us, we will go inside. Are you comfortable here?'

'We are fine,' Acuna said, also standing. My parents turned to go into the house. 'Excuse me, Señora,' Acuna said, 'but a thought has just struck me.'

It was shocking that he had spoken directly to my mother. It was a terrible disrespect to my father. Yet Acuna spoke with such softness that it didn't seem like that. All the same, I flinched.

'Señora, you may be right. Perhaps your son is not a goalkeeper. He may look like one now, but in two years who knows? Professional football is not an easy way of life, no matter what the TV tells you. DSJ signs about twenty young men every year. Most of them do not make it. In two years from now your son may come back here, knowing that football is not his future. But you will have ten thousand dollars all the same. And I am sure that you have worked out how much it would cost to send your son to college.'

I lifted my head and looked at my parents. It was obvious to me that Acuna's words had struck a chord in my mother. The way she simply nodded, looking directly at him, rather than turning away to continue into the house, told me that. And besides, a famous and handsome man had spoken to her, appealed to her, directly and respectfully. That was not an everyday thing. By contrast, my father looked lost, baffled. He looked like a general whose troops had deserted him, leaving him to face the enemy alone. It hurt my heart to look at his face. My mother lowered her head and went inside. My father followed her.

Señora da Silva drank a little water. Then she looked right at me for the first time. She flashed me a smile, probably one she had rehearsed in front of a mirror. It was very good.

'For such a talented and versatile young man, you are remarkably quiet,' she said. 'But, of course, this is difficult for you. I understand that. It seems that your parents have different ambitions for you. All the same, I would like to know what you think.'

What did I think? I thought that the world had suddenly become huge. I thought that my life was bursting at the seams. I thought that it was the Keeper who explained things, not me. And yet I had to say something.

'I am very honoured that you came all this way to watch me play, Señora,' I said. A pathetic answer.

She made a dismissive sound – *tcherr!* – and leant back, tapping her nails on the table. Then she leant forward and said, 'What are you? Are you a scientist, some sort of expert in this forest of yours? Are you an engineer? Or are you a goalkeeper? Come, your parents are inside. Speak for yourself.'

I looked down at the table and concentrated on an ant which was struggling with a drop of spilt cordial. It was hard to tell if the ant was trying to carry the sugary liquid away or escape from the sweet stickiness that had trapped its legs.

Then Larsson put his hand across the table and flicked the ant away with his finger. 'You are not stuck, my friend,' he said. 'You know the answer to that question. There is only one answer.'

'I think I am a goalkeeper,' I said.

Señora da Silva raised her sculptured eyebrows. 'Think?' she asked. 'Only *think?*'

'I am a keeper,' I said. 'I have no choice in the matter.'

'No,' Acuna said. 'I watched you today, and I have to say I think you are right. You have no choice. You are a keeper, at least for the time being. It is hard to imagine you being better at anything else.'

My parents came out of the house. My mother sat once more against the wall. My father sat in the chair facing Señora da Silva. His face was full of trouble. It took some seconds for him to be able to speak.

'Señora. My wife and I have discussed what you say. My wife's opinion is that I should sign this paper of yours. She does not want our son to be a footballer, I want you to understand that. You already know what she wants for him. But yes, it all comes down to money. Everything does, always.'

Señora da Silva regarded my father seriously, nodding her head slightly as though she too found this simple truth regrettable. Then she produced a slender silver pen from the inside pocket of her leather jacket and placed it and the contract in front of my father. Instead of picking up the pen, my father put his elbows on the table and combed his fingers through his thinning frizzy hair.

'I am sorry,' he said. 'I find this very hard. My son has a good job. He is good at tool shop. Estevan and all the others say so. What is football, compared to this? OK, he can keep goal, Saturdays. But he is my only son. How can I say OK, take him away to San Juan, take him from us? We have no telephone, nothing. I do not know what it would be like not to have him here. I cannot imagine it. When would we see him? And in San Juan, who would care for him and protect him? Forgive me, Señor, Señora. This is so, so … surprising. I cannot sign anything here and now. I need time to think.'

My feelings at that moment were very complicated. I was proud of my father. He was alone in this situation, in which everyone except him wanted the same thing. Bravery was not something that came naturally to him. But he was standing – or, rather, sitting – alone. And he was talking, perhaps for the first time, about how much he loved me, and wanted me to stay near him. And yet, inside, I was gasping with impatience. I wanted, desperately wanted, him to shut up and sign the contract. The door to my real life was open, and my father stood in front of it, blocking it. I loved him and hated him at the same time.

There was then a stalemate, another painful silence. It was broken by a brisk tapping noise, a stick banging against the wall of the house. Uncle Feliciano came round the corner into the light, blinking like a stunned owl. Señora da Silva slumped back in her chair, thinking, I suppose, that here was another member of this dumb jungle family coming to make life difficult.

Uncle Feliciano approached the table. He seemed to see only the person he spoke to.

'Milton Acuna,' he said. 'You were one hell of a player. I am glad that you have cut your hair. You always looked like a *bandido*, or, worse, a hippy. That goal you scored against Argentina in sixty-eight was the best I ever saw. You danced round three defenders, and no one has ever explained how you kept the ball. Then that shot. I hope my sister's son has made you welcome to this house.'

'Four,' Acuna said. 'It was four defenders.'

Uncle Feliciano scuttled sideways, like a crab, to my chair and nudged me out of it. I went and leant against the wall. He made a big business of getting settled. He still seemed unaware of anyone other than Acuna.

'Yes, it was four. Forgive me, my memory is old. But the shot was beautiful, and I think you took it with your left foot, although you are a right-footed player. Am I correct?'

Acuna might have smiled, enjoying the praise, but he didn't. Instead, he looked at Uncle Feliciano like a suspect being interrogated by a sly policeman. He said nothing. Uncle helped himself to the glass of cordial that Señora da Silva had refused.

'It is a very great pleasure to meet you, Señor Acuna,' he said. 'Unless my old brain is playing tricks on me, that Argentine goalie was Perez – am I right?'

Acuna nodded.

'A great keeper, but you fooled him. I have watched that goal, oh, maybe fifty times on television. It is used for adverts, these days. They use your goal to sell underpants, Señor Acuna, did you know that?'

Something like a smile did now drift across Acuna's face.

'And Perez should have stood up to your shot and stopped it,' said my uncle. 'Instead of that, he went down to his right because he had decided that you would use your right foot to put the ball inside his right post. And you drifted it over him with the outside of your left foot. Ten minutes later you had the Copa America in your hands.'

Uncle Feliciano fell silent but kept his eyes fixed on Acuna's. Acuna said, 'With respect, Señor, is there some point to all this?'

'Oh yes, Señor Acuna. You have watched this boy here only once. But tell me: would that shot have beaten this kid? Or would he have read you?'

Acuna looked at me. 'I think he would have stopped it,' he said.

Uncle Feliciano lifted his stick and slapped it down on the contract. Señora da Silva's pen jumped from the surface. The cordial glasses rattled. My uncle leant into my father's face and said, 'Sign this damn thing. Give the boy his life. He is ready.'"

"I KNEW EVERY inch of the path, of course, and all its tricks – the places where it hid itself, pretended to fade away, the places where the forest stretched its fingers out to lash at your eyes, where roots snaked out to trip you up. But I had never gone in there at night before, and I had never run so desperately towards the clearing. Here and there tiny splashes of silver light lay on the forest floor like coins, and now and again I caught a glimpse of the fat-faced moon sliding through the canopy of branches way above me.

I was shaking, and soaked with sweat, when I stumbled into the clearing. I put my hands on my knees and dragged the air, always sharper and cleaner here, into my lungs. The clearing was drenched in cold light. The moon had come to a stop overhead. Everything was divided into just two colours: brilliant silver and an inky blue-black. The silence was like something solid you could lean against, and rest, and recover from miracles.

I did not expect the Keeper to be there. Whatever and whoever he was, he seemed to depend on daylight. I was quite sure he would not materialize at night. When my breathing had steadied, I straightened up.

He was standing in the goalmouth, his back against the right post, arms folded over his chest, staring at the ground. No football. My heart lurched like a truck going over a rut in the road. It was as hard as it had ever been to walk towards him. I stopped at the penalty spot.

'It has happened, then,' he said. It was not a question. So I didn't answer.

He began to pace. He touched the upright nearest him, walked to the other, touched that, walked back, touched. Walked back. I waited. At last he faced me.

'Because of what I am,' he said, 'I have almost forgotten what it is like to be afraid. I should have taught you more about fear.'

'I have signed for DSJ,' I said. 'Why are you talking about fear? I am not afraid. I am happy. Do not spoil this, please.'

He looked at me. From within the shadow of his face two tiny lights shone, like distant stars in deepest space.

I said, 'No, that's not true. I am afraid. I am afraid of not coming here. I do not know what I will do without you.' I was outraged to discover tears in my eyes.

The Keeper smiled. Actually smiled, like a living person. Tiny muscles reorganized his face. One more amazing thing to happen on one amazing day.

'What happened in the game this afternoon?'

I struggled with the question, then offered the simplest answer. 'I was beaten,' I said.

'By what?' demanded the Keeper. 'What made you vulnerable? What were you doing when that goal was stolen?'

I thought about it, went back to the game. 'I think I lost concentration. My head was not clear enough. I was reacting to one player. He told me tonight that his job was to put me on a roller coaster, and he did that. He was testing my temper.'

Then I remembered. 'Thank you for speaking to me then. It helped.'

He gave a slight nod.

'Also, I let the crowd get to me. They were expecting something to happen to me, and I let that affect me. They were much louder today. The noise disturbed me. Once or twice I could not tell if the roar was coming from inside me or from outside. I could not tell the difference.'

The Keeper studied my face for a moment. 'Yes,' he said, very quietly. 'As I said, I have not been able to show you everything. Perhaps I have not had enough time.' He walked to the edge of the clearing. 'Come here.'

The Keeper spread his right hand in front of my face, his fingers like the bars of a cage. Through them I saw the moon, which had somehow come down closer to us, hovering over one corner of the clearing, glaring at us, hard and blue.

'Watch. Do not blink.' He moved his hand very slowly from side to side. The moon flashed, died, flashed again as his fingers moved across it. I had the sensation of shrinking and also of floating. His voice was now distant and tiny and crystal clear: 'Follow my hand with your eyes. Do not blink.' I turned as his hand moved, tracking across the clearing. His hand brought the moon with it. No, that's not quite right. His hand brought *another* moon with it, leaving the first where it was. It was as if he had slid one disc of light from behind the other. His hand carried this other moon to the second corner of the clearing, and stopped. Again the clear distant voice: 'Do not stop watching. Follow.' His hand moved on, and from his spread fingers a third moon appeared, slipping from behind the second; at the final corner of the clearing his hand paused again. When there were four moons, one at each corner, he shook his hand as if he had cramp, or as if a fly had settled on it. And I felt restored to my normal size; my feet were once more firmly on the grass. The light that now flooded the clearing was almost blinding. The four moons blazing down on us printed my shadow four times on the turf like the spokes of a wheel with me at the centre. The Keeper had no shadow at all.

He stood facing the wall of the jungle for a moment.

Then he stretched out his right arm, turned, and began to run, quite slowly. The trees he passed and gestured at with his outstretched arm began to move. Slowly, at first. Silver leaves and silver twigs and silver branches and ink-black shadows bent towards him as he passed, as if wanting to go with him. The Keeper circled the clearing twice, and by the time he returned to where I was standing the whole forest was gripped by the storm that he had summoned up. It hissed like a million snakes, howled like a million monkeys, threatened to tear itself to pieces and whirl into the sky. Yet in the clearing itself the air was eerily still. We seemed to be in the eye of a cyclone.

I fell to my knees. I wanted to claw my way into the earth to escape the terrible flood of moonlight and the screaming rage of the forest. And then, like a knife cutting through everything, the Keeper's voice: 'Get up. Stand. Go to the goalmouth.'

Dazed, shaking, I went. The posts and the ancient net were electric blue in the moonglare. I narrowed my eyes against the storm and the light and saw the shifting shape of the Keeper placing a football at his feet. He moved, a glowing silhouette, and the ball grew larger, larger, and then was past me before I could move. Despite the uproar of the forest, I heard the whisper as it struck the net behind me. Dumbly, I turned to pick the ball up from the back of the goal and found it had disappeared. Baffled, I faced the Keeper again – once more he had the ball at his feet, and once more he struck it, and once more it swelled and flew past me. I stood straight and faced him.

'What is your problem?' he asked me through the barrier of noise and motion.

I was unable to speak. I did not think I could make myself heard.

The ball was once again at his feet. He ran it towards me, his feet flickering. He made as if to shoot, dropping his right shoulder, putting his weight on his right foot.

'Call!' he yelled.

I managed to unstick my tongue from the roof of my mouth. 'Low, left!' I screamed hoarsely.

The ball did not come at me because he had put his foot on it and stopped it dead. He turned his back on me, took the ball back several paces and came at me again, tracking slightly to my left. I squinted into the fierce light and watched him closely.

'Call!'

'Low left again!' I moved to make the save, but once again he stopped the ball dead; and then turned instantly, knocked the ball slightly to his right, and struck it cleanly at the top-right corner of my goal. Two moons blinded me; I had to imagine the route of the ball because I could not see it. Somehow I struggled through the screaming air and tipped the ball over the bar. It vanished and was back at the Keeper's feet by the time I had stood up. But now he ran at me, feinting this way and that, evading imagined or ghostly defenders, his route very unpredictable. I understood that this was no longer practice. He intended to beat me. The invisible crowd howling from the forest faded into almost nothing. In the burning light I could see only the ball and the magician controlling it. He went out to my right, stopped the ball and dragged it back, set his body for a left-footed shot at the right of my goal, turned again, and then ran at me, chipping the ball up slightly: he was going for a half-volley from close range.

I sprang out of the goalmouth, but before I could reach him, the Keeper drew his right leg back to make the shot; the ball seemed to hover just above the silver grass, just beyond my reach. I flung myself sideways. I could not guess the angle the Keeper was going for, so I made myself as big as I could, spreading myself across his line of fire. I heard the hollow bang of his boot striking the ball. It hit my chest with heart-stopping force. I tried to smother it with my arms, got a hand to it, but crashed onto the turf at that instant. I saw the Keeper almost on me, a huge silhouette against the glaring moons, and braced myself for the impact. There was none. He went either over me or through me. I got to my knees, looking around desperately for the ball. It was rolling slowly away from me, about two metres away. The Keeper had come to a halt almost in the goalmouth, and had turned and thrown his weight forward ready to knock the ball into the net. He was as near to it as I was. I crouched and sprang, pure reflex. I was at full stretch when my hands reached the ball, and his boots were centimetres from my face. I turned onto my side, away from him, and wrapped myself around the ball. There was one more roaring surge of noise from the forest around us; then, in a moment, it faded and vanished.

The silence was shocking, and wonderful. I felt like a man who had been drowning but had bobbed up through the surface of the sea into the air again. I could hear the rasping of my breath, the beating of my heart, the creak of the leather ball beneath my fingers. I lifted my head.

The clearing seemed very dark in the pale light of the single moon that hung above me. The trees around the clearing were perfectly still. The Keeper was standing on the goal-line, his arms folded on his chest.

'Good,' he said. 'A good save. Are you OK?'

I nodded and stood up. My knees were shaky.

'Football is not often a quiet game,' he said.

I think I laughed.

'The trick,' he said, 'is to let the noise flow through you. Like a tree allows the wind to pass through its leaves and branches. In this way it remains standing, even though the wind is much stronger than the tree is.'

My breathing settled, and I was back in the real world again. I remembered what had taken place at my house earlier, and a great anxiety filled me.

'I am not ready,' I said. 'I have so much still to learn.'

'Not from me.'

This seemed such a cold and final thing to say. I suppose I must have looked as if I had been slapped in the face.

His voice softened a little. 'There are things that you cannot learn here, in this secret little field of ours. You have to go out into the world, and play your game under lights even brighter than those you played under tonight, and against noise that will make what you heard tonight seem like a whisper. You will be afraid, of course. Only very stupid people never feel fear. But you have courage, and you know you are good.' He gazed around at the trees, and it seemed to me that he faded slightly; his shape became vague for a second. 'Besides,' he said, 'who knows how long this place can survive? The forest is being killed, tree by tree. Every minute another hectare vanishes. Do you think that we can resist those machines of yours, the ones you work so hard to keep functioning?'

'I will not be doing that any more.'

'No, and I am glad of that, at least. When will you leave?'

'Tomorrow. The people from Deportivo are picking me up at nine o'clock.'

There was a question I needed to ask but I hardly knew how to word it. I stumbled through it somehow.

'I know you are there at the camp when I play. Will you be there in San Juan? Will I know you are there? Will you help me?'

Instead of answering he held out his hands. I gave him

the ball, and he stared at it like a gypsy reading futures in a crystal ball.

'You must understand,' he said, 'that it is very difficult for me to leave the forest. I have been trying to leave for a very long time.'

He lifted his face and once again I glimpsed those specks of light, the distant stars, that were perhaps his eyes.

'That is why I called you here,' he said. 'To help me leave. To end the waiting.'

'So you can leave now? You'll be with me at San Juan?'

'No. I will be here. My wait is not yet over.'

'I still don't understand,' I said. 'Are you saying that you will be here if I need you?'

Something happened to his face that may have been another smile.

'Actually,' he said, 'it is I who need you.'

He walked away from me, towards the edge of the clearing. Bouncing the ball, catching it, bouncing it again.

'Don't go,' I said.

He stopped but kept his back to me, still bouncing and catching the ball like a basketball player.

'I will come back,' I said.

He turned.

'We are depending on it,' he said.

The light failed. I looked up and saw a narrow cloud the shape of a knife blade cut the moon in half. When I looked down again he had gone."

S OMETHING ODD WAS happening to Paul Faustino. As a
journalist, he was used to being lied to. It came with the
job. For that reason, he was good at recognizing liars. He
knew too well the heightened sincerity in a man's voice that
heralded a lie. He could spot the tiny swivel in the eye, the
slightly exaggerated body language which told him that
truth was being shown the door. But during the several
hours he had now spent with El Gato he had detected none
of these signals. Worse, the shine he now saw in the goalkeeper's eyes had nothing to do with the light reflected
from the gold trophy on the table. It was caused by tears.
The man was trying not to cry. Faustino found himself
briefly considering the outrageous possibility that he was
being told the truth. He cleared his throat.

"Gato? Gato, have you just described your last meeting
with the Keeper?"

"Yes."

"You never saw him again?"

"No," the goalkeeper said. "Well, yes, I saw him – I think I saw him – in San Juan. But I've never met him or spoken to him since that night in the forest."

"You've never been back to look for him?" Faustino asked.

"Yes. Just once."

"And?"

El Gato massaged his face with his hands then sat straighter in his chair. "It was the day after my father's funeral. I waited until the quiet part of the afternoon and found the track I had always taken into the forest. It led nowhere. The curtain of leaves that I expected to open onto the clearing now opened onto even denser vegetation. I blundered around like a stupid tourist for two hours, but the clearing had disappeared. There was no sign at all of where it might have been."

Faustino considered this. The man had, then, suffered two losses at the same time. A double bereavement. But time was getting on, so he said, "Tell me about San Juan, Gato. What was it like for a fifteen-year-old boy from the jungle to find himself in the big city?"

"I saw ordinary things for the first time. Traffic lights, policemen, umbrellas, burger bars. Shops that sold just one thing – watches, or shoes, or books. Crowds of people walking to work along pavements. Roads and pavements astounded me. I thought of the millions of tons of concrete and stone beneath the city's feet, and the amount of human work that had put it all there. I saw children sleeping on the streets."

"Where did you live, Gato?"

"I went to live with Cesar Fabian and his wife," Gato said. "Cesar was, still is, a physio at DSJ. A lovely man. A lovely couple. I shared a room in their house with another boy, another junior. He didn't stay though. He left after six weeks, because he couldn't deal with his homesickness."

Faustino said, "And you, Gato? You were not homesick?"

It was as if the great goalkeeper had not considered this question before. After a pause he said, "No. Not really. I felt sort of unreal, as if I were in a dream. But it was a good dream, not a bad one."

Gato was silent for a moment, and then he said, "But there was one thing that did make me feel homesick. If that's the word for it. Sad, confused, anyway. Do you know San Juan, Paul?"

Faustino pulled a face. "Unfortunately, yes," he said. "It stinks. I prefer cities that know the difference between a sewer and a street."

The keeper laughed. "That's the Old City you're talking about, the port. But between the Old City and the New City there's what people in San Juan call the Park. About a hundred years ago the Old City got too small for all the people who swarmed in it, so they hacked away the forest behind the port and started to build the New City. But they decided to leave a chunk of the forest alone, a sort of breathing space between the filthy Old City and the clean New City. They built a cage of railings around it. So now there is a piece – a very big piece, in fact – of wilderness imprisoned within the city. Monkeys, birds, butterflies, live in this prison. That's where Cesar and his wife took me on my second day in San Juan. They thought I'd be glad to see it. In fact, the Park was like a joke about my life and my father's life. A fake wilderness with tarmac paths and picnic tables and litter. It made me squirm like a worm on a hook. All the same, I went there quite often, just to remind myself of what the sky looks like when you see it through a web of trees. And every time I went there, yes, I did feel homesick."

Faustino thought, Yes, I could make something of this. A piece to touch the reader's heart. Need more facts, though. So he said, "Tell me about your day-to-day life in San Juan, Gato. You were under contract. What did you have to do? What do kids who belong to football clubs actually do?"

"To my great surprise," Gato said, "we went to school. Every morning, five days a week."

"Football school?"

"No, proper school. Maths, writing, science, history. My mother was delighted when I wrote and told her this. She had thought that football and education were enemies.

She'd thought that when my father wrote his slow name on Señora da Silva's contract he had sentenced me to two years of stupidity. She was very happy to learn from me that I was receiving an education, free."

"And were you?"

"No. The year I went to DSJ there were eighteen other boys like me. Boys from all over the country. From small towns, from city slums, from the kind of backwoods place I was from. Of those eighteen, ten had never held books in their hands. They could have recited the names of the Boca Juniors side of 1976, but couldn't have read those same names from a piece of paper. I sat in classes where we were taught the alphabet."

Faustino could imagine a big smart kid sitting in a schoolroom trying not to look too clever while his classmates grappled with the simplest structures of their own language.

"So did you learn anything?"

"Yes. I learnt to be quiet. I learnt to watch. I learnt that it was perfectly possible for someone to be an idiot in the classroom and a genius on the pitch."

Faustino, smoking, considered this for a moment or two. Then he said, "And after school?"

Gato said, "Two afternoons a week we worked as drudges. Cleaning, preparing kit, following the groundsmen around, carrying gear from one place to another, being yelled at, sweeping, running errands. Three afternoons a week we trained. Hard. Milton Acuna was in charge of the Junior training programme, and he didn't pull any punches. He was fierce. I was OK with this, because he wasn't as hard as the Keeper. Some of the other boys suffered though."

"Were you the only keeper among the Juniors?"

"That year, yes. That meant that sometimes I worked with the first team goalie, Pablo Laval, and also with his understudy, Ramos."

Faustino leant back in his chair so that his face went out of the lamplight. "I knew Pablo quite well," he said. "In fact, he was the first person who told me about you. He was a fine keeper. Did you get on with him? I ask this because you took his place in the DSJ side, and he never got it back. That must have been tough on him."

"I would not have taken his place if he hadn't fractured his collarbone in a Cup-tie against Palominas. Pablo was excellent. It was an education, watching him play. He was very generous towards me. I had no problem with Pablo."

Faustino leant forward and said, "I interviewed Pablo Laval when he announced his retirement. I remember what he said. He said, 'At half-time, in that first senior game the kid Gato played, I knew I was finished. I saw that the lad knew more about keeping goal than I ever would. I knew I'd never get my place back.' OK, he was thirty-two years old, but he didn't have to quit. But he did, right then. And it must have hurt him."

El Gato then also leant into the light and looked his friend square in the face. "I tell you again, Paul: I had no problem with Pablo. After that game, he took me down to the locker room and gave me his shirt. It was a sort of ritual. He said that the number 1 was mine now. I said that I had only played one good game, and he had played hundreds. I said that I could not take the shirt. But you know Pablo. He doesn't take no for an answer. He made me take off my number 23 shirt and put on his. While my head was still inside the shirt I heard the locker-room door slam. I pulled the shirt down over my head and turned round to look where Pablo was looking. It was Ramos, still in the full kit he had been wearing as he'd sat on the substitutes' bench."

"Ah," Faustino said, "Ramos. I was going to ask. You were, what, just sixteen at the time? The youngest team member ever to play for the DSJ Seniors. And Ramos had been Pablo's deputy for something like two years, am I right? And you'd been preferred to him. I take it he was not best pleased."

"He hated me," Gato said flatly.

"Fancy that," said Faustino.

"As a keeper, Ramos was OK. But he was moody, and often reckless. He had a mean streak. He'd earned a lot of yellow cards in a fairly short career. And when he came into the locker room and saw me in Pablo's shirt he went off like a volcano. I think he'd have killed me if Pablo, with his one good arm, hadn't grabbed him by the throat and pinned him against the wall."

Gato paused, remembering. "In fact, not long after that, he did try to kill me. To have me killed, anyway."

Faustino sat up straight. "You're kidding."

"You must not print this, Paul, because I couldn't prove it. But I know it was Ramos."

"What happened?"

"Well," El Gato said, "I kept my place in the side. I was all over the newspapers. Ramos was insane with resentment. He had more poison in him than a pit viper. When one newspaper interviewed me, I was careful to say good things about him, and that made matters worse, if anything. Anyway, one Sunday I went into the city by myself and went into the Park. The cleared areas were full of families having picnics. I guess I was feeling lonely. I walked a long way into the trees along narrow paths until I could no longer hear voices. I started to feel both at home and homesick.

I stopped and leant against the mossy ribs of a great cinchona tree and peered into the beautiful gloom of this imprisoned jungle. I was thinking about the Keeper, of course, imagining him, waiting... And then I saw him. I saw him begin to materialize out of the dark ferns and creepers. I was overjoyed, just for a second or two. But then I saw that he was in great distress. He seemed to be struggling to make himself real, to stay visible. He flickered in and out of focus, never quite there, like a film projected onto glass. I could see, though, that he was pointing – at me, I thought – and that his mouth was moving, twisting. He was trying desperately to speak, but no words came. I don't understand how, but I suddenly realized that he was trying to warn me. I pushed away from the tree and turned, fast.

The two guys were about ten metres from me. They weren't much more than kids, really. A year or two older than me. Pale, skinny kids with long hair. They wouldn't have been particularly frightening if it hadn't been for the long narrow-bladed knives they were carrying. We faced each other, frozen, for a heartbeat. Then they came at me, and I started to run. I ran off the path straight into the dark heart of the forest. Something, some memory or instinct, must have kept me from stumbling. They came in there after me, but not very far. They were city boys and wouldn't have liked cobwebs on their faces or the thought of slithery things in dark places. Their crashing and cursing faded away behind me. Eventually I felt safe enough to stop. When my heart and breathing had steadied, I moved cautiously towards the distant sound of traffic. After twenty minutes I came out onto the boulevard between the Park and the Old City."

"Hell's teeth," Faustino said. "And you reckon these guys weren't just ordinary muggers? Junkies? What makes you sure that Ramos had sent them after you?"

"When I reported for training on Monday afternoon,

Ramos was getting out of his car. The look on his face when he saw me told me everything. And he knew that I knew."

"What happened to him?"

"He was transferred before the end of the season," Gato said. "The last I heard, he was playing in Colombia. But that was years ago."

"And you remained DSJ first keeper for the rest of the season," Faustino said. "And as they say, the rest is history. I have it here."

He got up and went across his office, opened a door and flicked a light switch. Turning in his chair, El Gato saw that the door opened into a smaller room with no window. The two walls he could see were lined with shelves crammed with files and folders and scrapbooks and cardboard wallets stuffed with paper. Faustino said, "My colleagues call this the Paul Faustino Library of Useless Knowledge. They fail to understand that no knowledge is useless. They also fail to understand my filing system. That's because there isn't one." He disappeared into the room, then emerged again carrying three enormous, old-fashioned box files. Each one had a label on which *EL GATO* had been written with a fat felt-tipped pen.

"My God," the goalkeeper said.

"Oh, this isn't all of it," Faustino said. "The rest is on that computer there. One day I'll pay one of those nerds from downstairs to put all this on disk. Then I'll never be able to find anything, but it'll all be very well organized. This is the earlier stuff. Everything I could find over the years, some of it written by me. Those are the best bits, naturally."

Faustino rested his hand on the files. "These are in chronological order. Well, more or less." He flipped open the lid of the first file and riffled through the collection of newspaper clippings, press releases and pictures. Gato glimpsed a photo of the boy he had once been. "So," Faustino continued, "this is stuff about that first season of yours as the DSJ keeper. The team finished third. Best position for, what, a hundred years?"

"Twelve, actually," the keeper said, smiling.

"And at the end of the next season, champions. Amazing. You are voted National Player of the Year. And so it goes on. You sign for DSJ for a further two years."

Faustino stopped, looked up at Gato. "Why?" he asked. "There were bigger clubs wanting to buy you. Foreign clubs, too. Juventus, Chelsea, Atlético Madrid. But you chose to stay in godforsaken San Juan."

The big goalkeeper shrugged. "Milton Acuna was persuasive," he said. "He told me that yes, one day I should go to play in Europe, but that in his opinion I was too young. I respected him. And the club offered me good money. Besides, there was my family. I was not happy at the thought of half the world separating me from them."

This was not quite good enough for the journalist. "And

it was something to do with the Keeper, perhaps? You told me that in the San Juan Park, when he half appeared to you, he seemed to be struggling to get there. Did you think there was a limit to his range, or something like that? That if you went further away he wouldn't be able to reach you? Or maybe that he couldn't communicate with you if there wasn't a chunk of your beloved rainforest handy? Was that it?"

El Gato thought about this and eventually said, "Paul, the Keeper comes with me here." He touched his forehead with two fingers. "I haven't seen him in the flesh for years, as I have told you." He smiled. "Those are the wrong words, 'in the flesh', but you know what I mean."

Faustino looked hard at his friend and decided to drop the subject. He went back to the file.

"National Player of the Year the next season, too. DSJ come top of the championship, blah, blah, next season they win the Cup, blah, blah. Then, at the great age of twenty, you sign for Unita and go to Italy. And in your very first season Unita win the European Cup."

Faustino lifted away the top file and flipped open the next. He took out an eight by four glossy black and white photograph. "This," he said, "is, in my opinion, one of the great pictures of all time. I'll use it in the article."

The photograph showed Gato lifting the European Cup above his head. How young, how triumphant, he looked! The Cup – more like a huge vase, in fact – seemed to beam the flashes of a thousand cameras down onto the young keeper's face, giving it the radiance you normally see only in paintings of saints. A photo full of joy.

At the sight of the picture El Gato's face turned to stone. He pushed his chair back, went to the window and spread his huge hands on the pane. He stood like that for perhaps half a minute; then he put his hands into his pockets and leant his forehead against the glass.

Faustino looked at his friend's broad back and then down at the photo. What the hell was this, now? He reached towards the *stop* button of the tape recorder, then changed his mind. He waited a few moments and then simply said, "Gato?" The goalie didn't move. "Gato? I don't know what the problem is. Are you going to tell me?"

Gato turned his back on the window. "Do me a favour, Paul," he said. "Don't use that damned photo. I never want to see it again."

Faustino looked from his friend to the photograph, and could think of nothing to say.

The goalkeeper walked across Faustino's office and back again, then sat down in his chair. He didn't speak, so Faustino lit a cigarette, slowly, and said, "Tell me, please, my friend," blowing blue smoke into the yellow cone of the lamplight.

El Gato stared at the surface of the table and said, "That moment, that moment in that picture, was magical. Soon afterwards, it became bitter. We'd won the European Cup, and Giorgio Massini handed it straight to me. We had a wild time that night, believe me. It was well after eight o'clock when the TV and the papers and everyone had finished with us, and then we went out on the town. We flew back to Rome the following day, all of us a bit the worse for wear, but still very, very high. At the airport, we were met by two open-top buses painted in the Unita colours and paraded through the streets, Massini and me in the front of the first bus with the Cup. Amazing scenes. Flowers, clothes, banners, money thrown at us. Fantastic. We ended up at some flash hotel or other. We did a press conference, interviews, photos. After all of that, most of the players went to their homes, wives, families, girlfriends, whatever. I was exhausted. I decided to stay at the hotel. I ate some food in my room and went to bed."

Faustino had been at that press conference, but this did not seem the right moment to mention the fact.

"I slept like someone who had died," Gato continued, "so when the hammering at the door started at seven the next morning it took me some time to come round. I stumbled out of bed and opened the door. A small woman stood there, fiddling anxiously with a large bunch of keys. She spoke urgently to me in Italian, pointing to the telephone beside my bed. I'd pulled the plug out of the socket before I'd gone to sleep – I hadn't fancied reporters calling in the middle of the night. I plugged the lead back in and picked up the phone. Someone said something in Italian, then a

175

distant, distorted voice came through. I wasn't wide awake, and for just a moment I thought that it was the Keeper, even though the idea of him using a telephone made no sense at all. But there was an echo on the line, a shadow to the voice, that made me think it might be him, and although I knew the voice I didn't recognize it.

It said, 'Gato? Is that you, Gato? This is Ernst Hellman.' Hellman! Oddly enough, my initial thought was that I'd never known his first name.

I said something like, 'Señor Hellman, it is nice of you to call.' I thought he was phoning to congratulate me.

'Thank God,' Hellman said. 'It's taken me three hours and sixteen calls to find you.'

I began to get a nasty feeling, a sort of cold sickness.

'Is everything all right, Señor Hellman?'

Hellman didn't reply straight away. I listened to the sound, like the wind, in the phone. Then he said, in his blunt way, 'No. Listen, Gato. There has been an accident.'

Then I knew.

'My father.' It was all I could do to speak just those two words.

'Yah, Gato. Your father. It's a terrible thing, telling you this. This day, of all days. He is dead, Gato. He was killed this morning.'

So I went home. It took me sixty-two hours."

"AFTER THE FUNERAL, in a long conversation with Hellman, I found out what had happened, more or less.

The Cup final had been an evening game in Holland, so the live TV coverage back home had kicked off at about two in the afternoon. It was a Wednesday, but Hellman had given everyone the afternoon off. I imagine he'd done some impressive yelling into that phone of his to swing that with head office.

Several families in the town, including mine, had TV now, but of course the only place to be for the game was in the café, where they'd rigged up two extra sets, big ones. The men swarmed in, still in their work kit and filthy boots, yelling for beer. My father had pride of place, a chair in front of the TV nearest the bar. Some of the men were already half-cut by the time the priest squeezed his way through the crush and climbed onto a table. He made a little speech, saying that it was good to see so many men gathered in one place to witness something they were passionate about. He said he looked forward to the same thing happening in his church one day. But, he said, this was a great event for the town, and especially for one of its families. Then he said a prayer for me, warned the crowd about the dangers of drink, ordered a glass of red wine and settled down to watch the game.

Do you remember the game, Paul? You were there."

"Yes, I was there. What I remember is that you had a great game, and no one else did, really. It wasn't what you'd call a classic."

"No. For the first twenty-five minutes or so we concentrated on keeping possession of the ball, as did Real. There were several slow build-ups which came to nothing much. All I had to do was clear a few back-passes and watch a long-range shot go well wide of my goal. The crowd got very impatient. Back in the café, there was a great deal of expert opinion flying back and forth. According to Hellman, my father was silent, just nodding when he was spoken to. Hellman said that he looked very pale, and was visibly shaking with tension.

It was our captain, Massini, who woke the game up, if you remember. He cut out a rare sloppy pass close to the halfway line and set off on one of his great galloping runs. No one came to meet him; the Real defence retreated, keeping their marking very tight. Massini looked up, saw that the keeper, Ruiz, was busy screaming and pointing to his defenders, and took a chance. He shot from almost thirty yards out, and he hit the ball so fiercely that when it struck Ruiz's left-hand post I heard the impact through the howling of the crowd.

Massini's near miss should have inspired us; instead, it fired up Real. They went for us like wolves. Ernesto Pearson, their Argentine striker, was especially dangerous; he took our defence to pieces. I had to make six or seven saves in the last ten minutes of the first half.

It was during this period that men in the café started buying my father beers. He was not a drinker, my father. OK, he'd sometimes have a couple of beers on a Saturday night, but he'd always come home early and fall happily asleep after winding Nana up a bit. But that day in the café he was bought a beer for each of the saves I made. And he was so worked up that he drank them all.

Well, you know what happened, Paul. We scored in something like the sixty-fifth minute. We didn't mean to go on the defensive after that, but the Spanish gave us no choice. They came at us more and more desperately. It was like trying to beat back the sea. But we hung on. We won."

Faustino let out a little snort of laughter. "There are just a couple of small details you forgot to mention, my friend. The fact is that *you* won that game. You stopped two direct free kicks, one of which you cannot possibly have seen until it was almost past you. And you saved Pearson's penalty four minutes from the end. That's what killed Real."

"I think it also killed my father," the goalkeeper said. "If the game had ended differently it is likely that my father would still be alive."

"The word *if* can drive you mad, Gato. There should be a law against it. Tell me what actually happened."

"Well, you may remember that when Massini picked up the European Cup he didn't lift it above his head in triumph, which is what captains usually do. He handed it straight to me, and I lifted it. In the café, that image of me holding the Cup, the same one as that photograph, filled all three TV screens, and that's when my father was hoisted up onto a table. He was already fairly drunk, according to Hellman, and had to be supported by men holding his legs. He would have been embarrassed and overjoyed at the same time, and when he felt in that mixed-up state he had a habit of nodding his head like a donkey bothered by flies. I can imagine the scene. I am so angry at the old fool. So angry."

Paul Faustino stayed silent.

Gato, too, was silent for a moment, and then he continued. "Anyway, that's when the men started calling for *cachaza*."

"Ah," murmured Faustino. "The demon rum."

"That's the stuff. And this was the local rum, smooth as silk and vicious as a whip. My father never drank the stuff.

My mother wouldn't have it in the house, anyway. And here he was, reeling about on a tabletop with a glass of it in each hand, while the mob chanted his son's name.

Hellman left the café at this point, but he pieced together the rest of the story during the next two days. The celebrations in my honour went on for the rest of the afternoon. When my father eventually managed to get out of the door he instantly collapsed in the street as if he had been shot. This was, of course, very funny. A couple of guys brought a table from the café and placed it upside down next to my father. They heaped his body onto it, and then four men, all wearing blue shirts with my name and number, somehow got the table onto their shoulders and set off, wobbling dangerously, across the plaza in the general direction of our house. They were followed by a crowd of chanting, cheering drunks.

My mother was not delighted to have this drunken rabble of her son's fans turning up at her door. When she realized that the arms and legs dangling from the upturned table were her husband's she almost fainted. My grandmother, of course, assumed that my father was already a corpse and wailed horribly while beating one of the table-bearers about the head with a soup ladle.

My father was still alive, in fact. He didn't die until the following day. He was lifted off the table and put to bed. He came round, just for a while, about an hour later. He managed to drink some water, then slept right through until the morning. My mother was horrified to find him awake and getting dressed for work at six o'clock. He looked like hell. She begged him not to go. He said that he had never missed a day's work in his life – which was probably true – and didn't intend to start now. So he went.

There was light unbroken rain that morning, and the men huddled inside their ponchos in the back of the pickup. Most of them were in the same sort of state as my father, red-eyed and shaky. My father threw up twice. Another man took out a small bottle of clear greenish liquid and persuaded Father to drink some. Whatever this brew was, it seemed to do the trick. Hellman told me that when the truck reached the camp, my father seemed OK. The rest of the crew didn't, though, and Hellman was half-minded to send them all home. But my father said no, they'd be fine. He was the team boss, and he'd make sure everyone was careful. So Hellman said OK. He congratulated my father on my success and went back into his office. The crew got into their bright green waterproofs – my father's had a broad orange band across the back – and set out for the cutting. The rain was heavier by now.

My father's was one of three crews cutting trees on the upward slope of a long low hill. It was a new section, so the machines hadn't churned up the ground too much, but there were streams of tea-coloured water running down off the hill. After an hour the team had set everything up and felled a big hardwood. It was a good tree, worth the work.

The trunk was thicker than I am tall. The sawyers and the saw-monkeys went in and trimmed it. By now my father had started to look pretty sick again. What had happened, I think, was that whatever was in that green stuff had got him a bit drunk again, which is why he'd seemed so confident talking to Hellman. And when that wore off, he felt worse than ever. But he was stubborn, and wouldn't quit. The crew got the cables fixed to the great trunk of the tree. By now the ground along the sides of it had been mushed up by the loggers' feet and the saw-monkeys were slithering around and swearing, their waterproofs fouled with red mud. The winchman, a guy called Torres, started the winch motors and began taking up the slack so that the cables came up tight. It was at this point that my father came up to the winch. He looked terrible, and Torres told him so. My father told him not to worry, and to run the motors at slow speed; he didn't want the trunk coming fast down the slope in this sort of weather. Then my father walked off and disappeared. Torres told Hellman he reckoned the old man had gone off out of sight to throw up again, not wanting anyone to see him do it.

Torres ran the winch at slow speed and the cables tensed and twanged like the strings of a huge guitar. The trunk shifted and the mud beneath it made a sucking noise. Then the trunk stuck, somehow. Torres eased the motors off and on again, trying to get the thing moving, but nothing happened. He was worried, and peered through the drifting rain for my father, who was nowhere to be seen. So what Torres did was crank the winch motors up to half speed for five seconds, to try to jerk the trunk free. It worked. The trunk bucked slightly and then started to move down the slope. It came a bit quicker than Torres would have liked, but it was OK. Then everything went wrong. The tree skewed and slid sideways. The top end of it came slicing down the slope, cutting through the undergrowth like a blade through grass. Torres knew the cables wouldn't hold, so he hit the release button and let the trunk go where it wanted to go. It turned and tumbled and finally came to a stop about sixty metres to the right of where it was meant to end up. What stopped it was one of the shallow gullies that were spewing water down the slope. The trunk rolled right into it.

It took Torres and the crew another hour to reposition the winch and the cables and drag the tree down to the foot of the slope to where the tractors could get at it. Twice Torres sent saw-monkeys to find my father, but there was no sign of him. Then, when the trunk had been dragged out, one of the boys spotted my father's green and orange jacket half buried in the mud at the bottom of the gully. So he scrambled down to pick it up. He couldn't do it. The jacket wouldn't come free of the mud. So he braced his legs and grabbed the collar with both hands and heaved. It was when the back of my father's head lifted out of the sludge that the boy realized my father was still inside the jacket.

The big hardwood had rolled right onto him and crushed him face down into the gully where he'd gone to be sick. That's how he died."

Faustino pressed the *stop* button on the tape recorder.

E L GATO WAS leaning back in his chair, his arms stretched out in front of him, his fingertips resting on the edge of the table. He stared blindly at the World Cup. Faustino was content to let this grievous silence continue because he was busy thinking.

Faustino was not what you might call a sentimental man, but he was baffled by the calmness with which El Gato had related the story of his father's death. Just as, earlier, he had been baffled by the detached way he had described those ... *what*? Experiences? Hallucinations? His friend's coolness was, of course, one of the attributes that made him the best keeper in the world; but Faustino found himself wondering if such self-control was, well, *unnatural*. Sometimes he didn't seem to be living in quite the same world as everyone else.

On the other hand, there was no doubting the emotion

Gato had shown when he had spoken about parting from the Keeper. Faustino was struck by the contrast. The man who had just related the death of his own father so matter-of-factly had been on the verge of breaking down when he'd talked about saying goodbye to an apparition. This goalkeeper was a damn sight more complicated than any footballer had the right to be.

Still, Faustino had begun to see a way of handling the mass of stuff that he'd taped during the course of the night. Three articles, not one. The first one would have to be about the jungle and the Keeper. Gato would probably insist on that. But Faustino thought he could put a bit of spin on the story, just enough so that the readers might believe it while understanding that he, Faustino, didn't. The second article would deal with the logging camp and the death of Gato's father. Good, solid human interest stuff. The third would be Gato's view of the World Cup final. (And there was still that to do, dammit. It would be dawn soon. He hoped the goalkeeper still had enough steam in him to talk through the video of the game.) The more Faustino thought over this scheme, the more he liked it. A three-day running exclusive on the man who was, for the time being, anyway, the most famous person on the planet. Sales of *La Nación* up by at least thirty per cent. Selling the story around the world. His boss would love it. And getting three exclusives for the price of one, that was exactly her style, the cheapskate. Faustino began to consider the size of the bonus he might be able to screw out of her. He started to feel very cheerful.

As sadly as he could manage, Faustino said, "I had no idea your father died such a terrible death. I am so sorry."

Gato tipped his head in acknowledgement but said nothing.

Carefully, Faustino said, "I'm surprised that I knew nothing of it. Never read about it anywhere."

Gato smiled a little. "It happened in the middle of nowhere. Loggers get killed every day. The story didn't make the national papers. And I've never spoken about it. Until now."

"Can I use it?"

"Yes," Gato said. "I want you to."

Faustino did reasonably well at hiding his pleasure.

"But, Paul," Gato said, "we'll not use this, if you don't mind."

"This" was the photograph. Gato flipped it casually back into the box file and closed the lid. Then he tapped the third file and said, "So what's in this? Which bits of me have you got in here?"

"Stuff up to about ninety-eight, I think. Your coming back, the years with Coruna and Flamingos. Then everything is on hard disk. Even pictures, up to and including us – *you* – winning the World Cup."

"So," Gato said, "you think you have everything you need?"

Faustino's face was all pained apology. "There's one more thing I'd like to do. Something I've *got* to do, really. If you have the energy." He looked at his watch. "I tell you what, the canteen here starts serving breakfast in forty-five minutes. It's usually pretty good. If you can give me another three-quarters of an hour I'll take you down there and treat you to what they call the Full Works, which I've never managed to finish. Deal?"

"Sounds good," Gato said. "What do you need to do?"

"I've got the final on tape over there. I'd like to go through bits of it with you. Especially the penalty shootout, obviously. Is that OK?"

"Yes, sure." The keeper smiled. "In fact, there are a couple of things I'd like to see again. I didn't watch any of the replays."

"You didn't?" Faustino was incredulous. "There's been nothing on the telly since. You must have seen it."

"No."

"You amaze me, you really do. OK, drag that chair over. The video is ready to run."

The two men arranged their chairs in front of a big flat-screen TV. Faustino picked up a remote control and thumbed a couple of buttons. The room was swept by sound, the German national anthem against wave after wave of roaring from the crowd packed into the vast bowl of the stadium. The pictures came from a hand-held camera tracking along the faces of the German team.

Faustino said, "We don't want to watch this, I presume. This machine has a really quick fast-forward. Shall we watch the Masinas goal that put us one up?"

"No," El Gato said. "Let's skip to the second half, when Lindenau scored the equalizer. I'd like to see that."

Faustino looked sideways at his friend. "You want to watch yourself being beaten?"

"Yes," El Gato said. "It doesn't happen that often, after all." And he laughed.

So Faustino pressed a button on the remote, and tiny players ran frenziedly around the screen. After a while, adverts, loud and lurid, flashed across the screen, followed by men gabbling in a studio. Half-time. Then more crazed rushing about by players in white shirts and purple and gold shirts.

"Here it is," Faustino said, stabbing the remote.

The video steadied and slowed. The screen showed the German striker, Lindenau, receiving the ball, a long pass that came over his shoulder. Gato said, "Let's go back a bit. Walter Graaf, their keeper, does something fantastic just before this."

Faustino rewound. Players ran frantically backwards. The ball went the wrong way, returning to each player who kicked it. Faustino hit another button and time started going the right way again.

"Look at this," Gato said. "Graaf is a great keeper.

I've played against him many times. He's steady as a rock. But watch this bit. He does something none of us expected him to do."

On the screen Germany were defending desperately. They were one down with barely twenty minutes left. They needed to score.

"Look," Gato said, pointing at the screen. "Here, here. The German defender, Effenberg, gets the ball but has no choices. He's hemmed in, between the touchline and Graaf's penalty area. So he passes back to Graaf. Now, nine times out of ten Walter will choose to hoof the ball up the field to give his defence time to reorganize. We thought that was what he would do here. So the players closing Effenberg down turn around, and back off him. But what does Graaf do? Look, here it comes. Walter shapes himself up to make the long clearance, but instead of doing that he plays a soft pass back to Effenberg. Crazy! Our attackers rush back at Effenberg. And look – our midfield turns and starts to move up as well, thinking that Graaf has done a mad thing. But what happens is that Walter rushes up to the edge of his penalty area so that he can take a return pass from Effenberg. This is the World Cup final, and Walter plays a one-two in front of his own goal. Fantastic! He carries the ball fifteen yards or so, then looks up and hits a fabulous diagonal pass towards Lindenau, who is just onside. Lindenau looks as if he'll take it on his chest, which would leave him with his back to my goal, but instead he dummies. He turns and lets the ball come over his shoulder. He leaves Carlos Santayana standing. He's only got me to beat, and twenty-five yards to do it in."

Faustino took a sideways look at Gato. The man was actually enjoying this! This was a video of how he almost lost the World Cup to Germany, and he was talking about it as if it had happened to someone else.

"It was obvious," El Gato said, "that Carlos couldn't catch Lindenau. So I had to come out and hope to get down onto the ball before Lindenau could get the shot in. At the same time, I knew that if I didn't make it he would chip the ball over me, and there was no cover on the goal-line."

"You come out of the goal like a guided missile," said Faustino, fixed on the screen. "Lindenau must have been terrified. He's only a little guy."

"I hoped to scare him," Gato said.

The two men watched the slow-motion replay of Lindenau lifting the ball over the diving, spread-eagled Gato and into the goal.

"You see what he does," Gato said, as the goal was replayed yet again. "He doesn't chip the ball at all. In the split second before I reach him he stops the ball dead – there, look – and spoons it over me with his right foot. So cool."

"OK," Faustino said. "The score is one–all at full time. No score in extra time. Shall we skip to the shoot-out now? Or do you want to look at the three incredible saves you made in the last fifteen minutes?"

"No. Let's get to the penalties."

The machine clunked and whirred. Crowd shots swept across the screen, then knots of players and coaches and substitutes formed and dissolved at lightning speed. Faustino thumbed the remote and the screen showed El Gato walking at normal speed into the goalmouth to face the first of the sequence of penalties which would decide who became World Champions. For a couple of seconds he was the only player in the frame, a solitary figure moving through an intense wall of sound. Then the camera pulled back to show Dieter Lindenau placing the ball on the penalty spot, fussing slightly about the way it sat on the turf, then turning away to take his run-up.

"He doesn't look at you," Faustino said. "Not even a glance at you. Or the goal."

El Gato smiled slightly. "He knows better than to do that. Also, look at the way he runs up – he changes direction very slightly. I couldn't read him or tempt him. I had to guess."

"You guessed right," Faustino said, as they watched the ball fly into the net just above the ground, just inside the right-side post, just beyond Gato's reach.

"Yes, I did. But I couldn't get to it. For me, that's the perfect place and the perfect height for a penalty. Ninety-nine players out of a hundred going for that shot will hit the ball with the inside of the foot, for accuracy. But that was a full-blooded drive he put past me, and it didn't rise ten centimetres. Very difficult to do. Great penalty."

Faustino paused the tape. "Tell me how you felt at that moment," he said.

The keeper shrugged. "Not desperate. I had four more chances, and I knew that Lindenau was their best penalty taker. The odds were still OK. But then everything changed."

"Yeah," Faustino muttered, pressing the button. "I've seen this a dozen times now, but I can still hardly bear to look."

On the screen Walter Graaf, in close-up, faces his first penalty. He stands quite still, hands on hips, while Babayo steps up to take it. As Babayo strikes the ball, with tremendous power, Graaf does a star-jump, arms high and apart. The ball flies just over the bar and vanishes into the howling, hysterical crowd. Babayo crouches, his head in his arms, devastated, crushed by the roar that fills the stadium.

"Poor Babo," said El Gato, quietly.

Faustino sat back in his chair and made a gesture of despair. "But he *never* does that," he said. "He'd scored every one of his last eighteen penalties. What the hell did he think he was doing?"

"Well," Gato said, "not even Babo had been under pressure like that before. He knew it was crucial, psychologically vital, that we also score with our first penalty. I'm not really surprised he missed. But it was then that I began to feel a little worm of fear start to eat me. It was possible, after all, that the World Cup would evade me a second time. A last time. It was an effort to push doubt aside as I waited for Tauber to take Germany's second penalty."

"And you saved it," Faustino said. "Here it is, look."

Gato watched himself fly to his right and palm Tauber's shot round the post.

"Great stop, my friend," rejoiced Faustino. "Tauber really hammered that one."

"It wasn't as hard as it looks. I offered him a tiny amount of extra space to my right, and he fell for it. And I could tell from the way he leant that he was going to hit it high."

"OK, now here comes Masinas," said Faustino, leaning closer to the screen. "This is good."

"Yes, a real captain's goal, this one. Look, just here, see? He bounces the ball a couple of times, casual as you like, on his way to the spot. And now he smiles at the referee and says something, and the ref smiles, too. But this little performance is for Graaf's benefit, really. And it works. Walter looks very edgy. Masinas just plops the ball down on the spot, doesn't tee it up or anything. Doesn't look at Walter at all. Here we go: look at that! Simple side-foot, sends Walter the wrong way, bang. One–one. Excellent. As if we were on the training pitch."

Paul Faustino looked at his friend and smiled to himself. Gato was watching this with all the simple pleasure and excitement of a teenage fan. Maybe he was a normal human being after all.

"So," Faustino said, focused back on the screen. "It's a penalty each and the game is still anyone's. Now you face Jan Maschler, the young midfielder. He'd had a good game, I think."

"Yes, and I'd never played against him before. This was only his third game for Germany. I was surprised that he'd been picked as one of the penalty takers. I didn't have any idea what to expect. He's a left-footed player, so naturally I figured that if he went for a power shot he would send it to my left, but if he shunted his weight in the run-up he would go for a side-foot to my right. I was wrong on both counts. Here it comes."

The two men watched the screen. To Faustino, it looked as though El Gato had left it very late to make the save, to make the fast dive to his right. But if he'd gone any sooner, he wouldn't have been able to block Maschler's shot with his legs, which was what he did. Maschler drove the ball straight at the very spot that Gato had left, at the dead centre of the goalmouth. But the keeper had timed it perfectly, Faustino realized. Watching the replay very closely, he saw that Gato seemed to float, just for a heartbeat, motionless in the air and look back along the length of his own body, somehow getting his legs to the ball, which cannoned off and away to the right of the goal.

Gato said, "Paul, if you say that was a lucky save I'll never speak to you again."

196

Faustino laughed. "After tonight," he said, "I'll never use the phrase 'lucky save' again, I promise you." He looked back at the video. "Here comes Paolo da Gama."

They watched da Gama place the ball very precisely on the penalty spot. The camera cut to Walter Graaf, who looked very confident, occupying his space.

Gato said, "I never doubted that Paolo would score. I'd have given him the first penalty if I'd been able to choose. He's always in the papers, being a playboy, a wild boy. But there's ice in his veins. Look how he does this. Walter doesn't have a ghost of a chance."

They watched da Gama's short, deceptive approach to the ball, his drop of the wrong shoulder, the way he slid the ball, not fast at all, into the net. Graaf hardly moved. Da Gama walked quietly off the screen, not celebrating, not milking the crowd's delirious applause, which came into Faustino's office so loud it seemed solid.

Once again the camera showed Gato in close-up on the goal-line; then the angle flicked to Tobias Mann, the enormous German defender, placing the ball for the fourth German penalty.

Then, as Mann walked away from the ball for a long run-up, Gato said, "Generally speaking, big fullbacks like Mann go for extreme power, rather than accuracy. And that's fair enough. After all, it's only twelve yards from the penalty spot to the goal-line, and someone like Mann can drive the ball that distance in less than a second. You don't have time to think about or calculate what to do. All you can do is hope to mess with the penalty taker's head. And the odds are always against the keeper because he isn't allowed to move until the kick is taken, as you know. So I cheated."

Faustino pressed the *pause* button. "You did what?"

"I cheated."

Both men were looking at the screen, which showed Mann frozen in a grim posture, hands on his hips, leaning forward slightly, staring defiantly into El Gato's face.

"What do you mean, you cheated?" Faustino wanted to know. "I've watched this over and over again, and I never saw you do anything wrong."

El Gato turned in his chair and looked at the journalist. "I'd noticed something about the referee," he said. "A tiny thing. He'd set everything up, check everything, confirm with his assistants, whistle to allow the kick. But, standing at the edge of the box, he'd always, at the very last moment, take his eyes off the keeper – whether it was me or Walter Graaf – and watch the kick. He didn't turn his head or anything obvious, but he'd flick his eyes at the ball for just that second as the penalty taker struck it. He couldn't help it. So I used it. Can you move the picture on a frame at a time?"

"Um, yeah, I think so," Faustino said, fumbling with the remote. "Here we are."

The screen now showed jerky stills of Tobias Mann

bearing down on the ball like a bull going for a matador. Then, briefly, just before the German struck, the camera cut to Gato.

"Freeze it there, Paul," Gato said.

Faustino stared at the image. "You've come off your line," he said. "About half a yard. And you're pointing, are you? Yes, you're pointing to the bottom-right corner of the goal. You're telling Mann where to put the shot!"

"Yes," Gato said, "and I've put my weight on my left foot, just to tempt him a bit more, make him think I'm going the other way."

"But I still don't get it," Faustino said, perplexed. "I mean, Mann was already committed to what he was going to do. You're not telling me, are you, that you persuaded him to try something different, right at the last moment?"

"Not really. But what I did was put another idea into his head, another possibility. Right up to that last split second his only thought was to blast the ball into the goal. Exactly where didn't matter that much. But then I put a second option into his head, too late for him to sort one from the other. I messed his mind a bit. That is why he misses."

The two men watched Mann's ferocious shot pass harmlessly wide of the right post.

Faustino, grinning, looked at Gato and said, "You know what? Of all the words I could use to describe you, *sneaky* is one I wouldn't have thought of. But that was downright sneaky. I'm shocked."

Gato didn't take his eyes from the screen. "I needed to win this game," he said.

"You must've thought you'd done it," Faustino said. "You'd saved three German penalties on the trot, which is incredible. We're two–one up, and it's our turn. If Fidelio scores, it's all over."

The camera cuts briefly to players not involved in this critical moment. Most of the Germans are sitting or crouching on the turf, not daring to watch. Lindenau is pacing back and forth in the centre-circle, making fierce little gestures and talking to himself. Tauber, the captain, with his arms folded, watches grimly as Fidelio picks up the ball and heads for the spot. The noise, the tidal roar of the crowd, is now almost unbearable.

"This is horrible," Faustino muttered.

"Graaf is superb here," El Gato said quietly. "I admire him so much for this. He knows he has to stop this one. And so far, he hasn't got a hand to a single one of our penalties. But he knows that Fidelio's fear is greater than his own. He knows that he will be forgiven if he is beaten by a penalty. But Fidelio isn't at all sure that *he* will be forgiven if he fails to win the World Cup with one. It's the most important kick, maybe the most important moment, of his life. And here, look, Walter stops on his way to the goal-line to fiddle with his gloves. Fidelio is already poised for his run-up, but he has to wait and watch. Just for five seconds, but that's another five seconds of dread. Walter stands on the line. He looks like someone waiting for a bus. Everything about him is telling Fidelio that he is not going to score."

On the screen Graaf hurls himself to his left to parry Fidelio's low shot, which has not been struck quite hard enough. Graaf deadens the ball with his forearms and it rolls aimlessly off the screen. The stadium explodes with noise and flares as thousands of German supporters roar out their anthem.

Faustino sighed, slumping back in his chair. "So Graaf keeps them alive," he said. "The score stays at two–one. Now it's down to you, Gato. Your last penalty of the five. Are you sure you want to watch it?"

"Yes. I think Rilke slices it, but I'd like to be sure."

Faustino stared at him. Any normal player, he thought, would hide in a dark cellar rather than relive a thing like this.

El Gato watched himself being beaten by the German midfielder without comment.

Faustino chose to say silent, too.

When the slow-motion replay came on, Gato leant forward closer to the screen. "I was right," he said. "Watch. Rilke's got the same sort of pressure on him that Fidelio had, but shows none of it. He starts his run-up, not a long one, six paces. He does a little shuffle, but I'm not buying it. He's going to go for top right, I'm sure, so I'm in the air almost before he hits the ball, because I know he's going to hit it very, very hard. And yes, he slices it, just a little bit. It cuts away from the top right slightly. Before I can adjust myself, the ball hits my shoulder and goes in off the underside of the bar."

He sounded, Faustino thought, *pleased.*

"OK," Faustino said, "two–two. After two and a quarter hours the whole game depends on Mano Elias." He paused the video as the slender winger walked slowly to the penalty spot. His purple and gold shirt looked too big for him. "What must it have felt like, being him?" Faustino wondered. "I can't imagine it. I don't *want* to imagine it. Twenty years old, and the whole damn world watching." The camera now showed small sections of the crowd in quick sequence. Faces, faces. Faces painted in greasy colours, faces strained with unbearable tension, eyes closed and teeth bared. A number of people praying; a section of German fans howling and pointing at Elias, trying to break his concentration, or his spirit; a woman frozen in what looked like pure terror, all her fingers stuffed into her mouth. Each shot, Faustino thought, looked like a painting of a madhouse in hell.

As if he had had the same thought Gato said, "Yes. Too much, too much. It was hell on earth at that moment. The noise was enough to make your ears bleed. I looked at Graaf and I looked at Mano, and I knew he wouldn't score. Knew it in my gut, like a chunk of ice."

He and Faustino watched Elias's shot hit Graaf's left

post and vanish off the screen. Faustino hurriedly jabbed the volume control on the remote as the German supporters erupted, and the camera cut between them and Elias, kneeling, wretched, wanting to die.

"Poor, poor kid," Faustino murmured. "As far as he's concerned, the entire world has just seen him throw away the World Cup. I imagine he just wants to plunge his head into the ground and keep it there."

With the sound off, the two men watched the preparations for the sudden death penalty shoot-out. They watched the two teams huddle and confer. There was an obvious difference between them.

"The Germans were much more up than we were," El Gato said quietly. "They'd come back from the dead. You can tell by looking at them that they had the feeling that, despite everything, they were destined to win. There, look: you can see Tauber and the German coach sorting out who takes the kicks, and no one is looking away. Lindenau is actually smiling. Now look at our squad."

The camera cut to the other half of the centre-circle. Masinas was moving among the players, desperately working to pump up morale. Yet Aldair and Gento were sitting staring at the ground, trying to be invisible. The coach, Badrenas, was holding Carlos Santayana by the arm, but Santayana was pulling away, shaking his head. Da Gama had his arms around Mano Elias, who was weeping uncontrollably.

"And you, my friend?" Faustino asked. "You look pretty

calm there. How were you feeling?"

El Gato laughed, but not in the way a man laughs at a joke. "Exhausted," he said, "absolutely exhausted. By now, it was pretty much three hours since we'd first walked out of the tunnel into that, that ... *cauldron* of noise and light. I felt used up. Worse, I was losing a fight with myself. I wanted that thing," he said, gesturing over his shoulder to the World Cup still burning in the lamplight, "more than I could imagine wanting anything else. I'd got within two games of it four years ago. Right through this game, right up to Elias's last kick, I'd hung onto the belief that I'd get it this time. Now I'd lost that certainty. A part of me believed that after all I'd done, I'd never get there. I was trying to kill that part of me, the doubting part. And I couldn't."

"And feeling like that," Faustino said, eyes on the screen, "you walk into the goal to face yet another penalty. Let me tell you, Gato, it doesn't look as if you have a shred of self-doubt in your body. If you were feeling the way you say you were, you deserve an Oscar as well as the Cup."

It was the German centre-back, Christian Klarsfeldt, who, through a terrifying barrage of roars and whistles and chants and howls, came forward to take the kick.

"The guy has guts," Faustino said. "He actually *volunteered* to take it."

"I know he did," said Gato. "And knowing that didn't help me one bit."

"What did you think he was going to do? Could you read him at all?"

"Not really," Gato said. "He's right-footed, and he doesn't score goals often. We'd watched loads of videos of the German players in the week before the game, of course. There wasn't one of Klarsfeldt taking a penalty. For all I knew, he'd never taken one. And look – he puts the ball down on the spot with his back to the goal."

"Yeah," Faustino said. "That's a weird thing to do. What the hell's that about?"

"He wants to show me his backside as he bends down to place the ball. It's a wind-up, an insult. It's a KMA."

"A what?"

Gato smiled and said, "Work it out, Paul. The K stands for Kiss."

Faustino laughed. "Right, right. You must have loved that."

"It's why I stopped the shot," Gato said.

The save, thinks Faustino, watching it, is pure genius. Even in slow motion, it's hard to work out how it's done. Klarsfeldt's run approaches the ball at an angle. Klarsfeldt has only one good foot, his right. The angle of the run suggests that he's going to turn his foot and send the shot hard to Gato's right. It also suggests that he'll lift the ball, because only experts like Lindenau can keep that kind of shot close to the grass. And Gato seems not to have worked this out. He commits himself in the wrong direction, throwing his weight onto his left foot. And Klarsfeldt glances up and sees this. So, Faustino realizes, if Klarsfeldt had intended to switch the shot, or had even just thought about it, that glimpse of Gato preparing to go to the left makes up his mind for him. He goes for the shot to the right. And what Gato does is power himself off the ground with the wrong leg, the left leg, into the flight of the ball. It looks clumsy, at first, then beautiful. The man *flies*. Gato's left arm is high; it looks as if he might catch onto the bar and swing from it. His right arm stretches; his huge hand opens and palms the ball over the bar.

Faustino looked at Gato and saw that he was smiling.

"No big deal, Paul. I was ninety per cent certain that Klarsfeldt would go for that particular shot. So was he. All I did was make it one hundred per cent certain for both of us. I just took doubt out of the equation."

On-screen, the camera roamed the crowd again. This time, the German supporters had their heads down. Faustino glimpsed a young couple, their faces painted in horizontal bands of black, red and gold, holding onto each other as if they were at a funeral, not a game of football. The camera cut to Walter Graaf as he walked towards the goalmouth. At the moment Graaf stopped and looked round in amazement, Faustino paused the video once again.

He said, "And at last we come to the final act. We come, Gato, to where you do that thing you do. The thing that everyone in this city, this country, and for all I know in the whole world, has been talking about these past two days."

Gato said nothing, apparently studying the German goalkeeper frozen on the screen.

Faustino said, "I need to know exactly what was going through your mind. Explain what you were thinking, what you were feeling."

Explain? Was it possible? Gato thought not. He would fail at this, this final thing. Because there was no way of saying it, or because he had said it already.

He had picked the ball up from where a boy in a tracksuit had rolled it, and didn't know why. His part in this was over now. But he held the ball and looked up the field and met Masinas's eyes. Masinas spoke, or rather his mouth moved. No words. No sound at all now. The vast rumble of the crowd withdrew, like a wave, and didn't come back. He was fifteen years old, walking as if in someone else's dream down through a mob of loggers, away from his astonished father, down to a rough football pitch, drawn with chalk on red dirt. There was a white spot twelve yards from the goalmouth upon which everything depended – his life and the lives and deaths of others. His legs took him there, past a man called Walter Graaf, who looked as if he were underwater but still trying to breathe. None of this mattered. He watched his hands put the ball down on the scuffed white spot, and at that moment the delayed wave came back, the wave of sound. Howling, birdcalls, the vibration in the air of a million million insects, the fierce irresistible wind hurling through the trees, hurling through him. He looked up at the hundred hard brilliant moons that burned down, cancelling out his shadow. The light and the sound were part of him and he was part of them. He looked into the goal where, a moment or an hour earlier, he had seen the drowning man, Graaf. A frightened boy, a boy called Cigüeña, stood there, all arms and legs and worried hands. The dark wall of a forest rose behind the boy. For a moment he felt sorry for Cigüeña, knowing that he would have to destroy him. He felt sorry for the boy because the path the ball was going to take went past him, straight into the web, and the boy couldn't see it. But he walked away from the ball anyway. He stood and looked into the boy's eyes, his own eyes, Graaf's eyes, and saw the fear in them. He made sure the fear was strong and deep-rooted before he began the run. The contact with the ball was beautiful; it was as if he made the flight into the net himself. In amongst the outrageous roar that came from the forest he heard the hiss of the ball against the net. Joy stretched inside him like a big cat after a kill, and the storm was saying, GATO! GATO!

"GATO?"

He was at the window, he realized. There was a dirty yellow tinge in the sky, and the night was separating into different kinds and depths of darkness. The stars were dying. Daybreak.

"Gato," Faustino said again. "Gato, you've said nothing. Come on. Sit down and talk to me. What am I going to write? What am I going to say?"

"Say that I did what I was meant to do," El Gato said.

Faustino looked at the man leaning against the window – the same man who, on the screen, was being carried on the shoulders of his fellow players with the World Cup in his hands.

"I'm tired," Gato said. "We can look at it again. We've all the time in the world."

Faustino kept his voice under control. "My friend, we

do *not* have all the time in the world."

He went back to his desk, sat down, and held up the three cassettes he had taped; there was a fourth still in the machine. As calmly as he could, he said, "We have talked all night. There is more than enough material here for three really strong stories. Have you any idea how much work I'll have to do to edit it all into shape? Even if I could go without sleep for another eighteen hours, I'd struggle to get the first piece into tomorrow's edition. So come on, please. Take me through that last penalty."

El Gato walked over to the table and sat down opposite Faustino. "We'll do it another time," he said.

Faustino lost it. "Christ Almighty, Gato! Haven't you been listening to me?"

The keeper didn't so much as blink. He said, "Haven't you been listening to *me*, Paul?"

"What?"

"Paul, I've told you things tonight that I've never dared speak about before. Not to anybody. Do you think I did that just to entertain your readers?"

Faustino suddenly looked like a man who'd found a snake in his car. "What the hell do you mean?"

Without shifting his eyes from the other man's, Gato said, "None of this, none of what I've told you tonight, is going to appear in your newspaper."

Faustino sprang up as if a stiff dose of electricity had been pumped through his chair. He put his hands flat on the table and leant into the lamplight, which, hitting his face from below, made him look ghoulish and crazed.

"*What?* What is this, Gato? Are you trying to tell me that all of this has been off the record? Is that it? Let me tell *you* something. It isn't. You agreed to this interview. You took the damned money. And I'm going to print it. There's nothing you can do to stop me."

The keeper lifted his hands, palms towards Faustino. "Paul, listen. I'm not trying to stop you publishing this. It's what I want you to do. Sit down. Please."

Faustino sat, eventually.

Gato said, "There's something I want you to think about."

Faustino was already thinking. He was thinking about lost sales. He was thinking about a lost bonus, about losing his job. He was thinking about lawsuits.

The goalkeeper said, "Paul, I want you to write a *book*."

"A what?"

"A book, Paul. Look, if all this ends up as a newspaper article, what will happen to it? It'll end up in the garbage with everything else. What will anybody learn from it?"

"What they will learn," Faustino said, with heat in his voice, "is a lot of fascinating stuff about the man who just won the World Cup. You have a problem with that?"

"Yes," said El Gato, "I do have a problem with that. Because no matter how well you write it, the story will be all about me. That's how you'll sell the papers, by putting my name all over the front of them. But the story I've been telling you tonight is not just about me. It's about all sorts of people. It's about animals, it's about the forest. Most of all it's about a ghost, a genius, a shaman, a conjuror, a non-existent person with no name. Do you think a newspaper that will end up in the garbage can is the best place for this?"

Faustino clamped his hands on the top of his head as if to stop it blowing off. "Gato, Gato," he said, "what the hell are you doing to me here? I'm a *journalist*. I draw a salary. Your agent and my boss made a deal, a deal for an exclusive interview. OK, I'm going to be a day late with it, but when she sees what I've got for her she might even like me a little bit. The damned crocodile might even love me. We could sell an extra million papers. And you are asking me not to give her any of it? You're crazy."

"If the story can sell a million papers, it might sell a million books," Gato said.

Faustino let out a long breath. Then he got up, picked up his cigarettes and lighter and walked to the brightening window. Facing it, he lit a cigarette. Three deep drags on it seemed to calm him.

"A ghost story. With me as the ghost writer. Is that it?"

The goalkeeper laughed. "Yes. That's good. I have a title: *Keeper*. What do you think?"

Still facing the window, Faustino shrugged. "It's OK. Whatever." He turned and faced the goalkeeper. "Look," he said, "let me be honest with you. I can't really get my head around the Keeper business. All that supernatural stuff... I know you're not lying to me. The problem is I don't believe you, either."

Still smiling, Gato said, "I know you don't. You've made that obvious."

"Have I?"

"Oh yes. But it doesn't matter. You're a good writer. You can write about things you don't believe in."

Paul Faustino had written three books. The last one had a nice photo of him on the back of the jacket. He knew how good it felt to hold something you'd written, something quite heavy, in your hand. Something with your name on the front cover. He wouldn't have admitted it to anyone, but he had several times typed his own name into an Internet search engine and been delighted when that photo popped onto the screen. But that had been an easy book to write, really. Just a collection of sports anecdotes strung together, stuff out of his files. El Gato seemed to be thinking about something entirely different. Faustino didn't know if he was up to it.

"I don't know," he said.

Gato waited. It was like tempting an opposing striker. He could sense that the journalist was just beginning to imagine himself as a Writer with a capital W. In a minute, Faustino would start to think about money. Gato had been in Faustino's car, an imported English Jaguar that needed expensive repairs every couple of months. And he knew enough about clothes to guess roughly what Paul had paid for the jacket he was wearing. So he helped his friend to think about the money.

"I don't suppose you've thought about this, Paul," he said, "but what do you reckon you'd get for this as a newspaper article? A nice bonus on top of your salary? A couple of thousand? I have no idea what we might make from the book, but..."

Faustino came back to the table. He exhaled smoke through pursed lips. He jabbed his cigarette into the ashtray.

"Yes, OK, maybe. I like the idea. But listen to me, please, Gato. You mention money. My paper is paying you a certain amount, I don't know or care how much, for this interview. I ask you, what am I going to say to my editor when I go up to her office and tell her there is no interview? That I am saving it all up for a book? She will skin me alive, Gato, and nail the skin to the wall as a warning to others. I can't do it."

"You will give her an interview. We'll do that as well."

"But Gato," Faustino said – or, to be more accurate, wailed – "she paid for an exclusive! Something special! You know what that means?"

"Sure I know what that means," Gato said. "And if I give you, and her, an exclusive, will you do the book with me?"

"What exclusive?"

"I'm quitting," said the world's best player.

"What do you mean?"

"Quitting. Retiring. We just watched my last game."

"What?" The word came out of Faustino like a hurt dog's yelp.

PAUL FAUSTINO HAD quit pacing and smoking and ruining his haircut with his hands, and had sat down again opposite the keeper.

"The first thing I need to ask you, Gato, is if you have told anyone this. Does your club know? And does Badrenas know? Badrenas is the best coach the national side has had in twenty years, but I don't like him and he doesn't like me. If he finds out about this from an article of mine he will have me killed. I really think he will."

"Badrenas knows," Gato said. "He has known for some time. I told him before the final. My club also knows. I confirmed my decision to Luis Ramerez before I came here last night."

Faustino became very agitated. "But if they know," he said, "they will have written press releases! Everyone will know!"

"No. They are expecting you to call them this morning. In the next couple of hours, in fact. Then they will confirm my decision, and only to you. They will give you the quotes you need. Tomorrow afternoon Badrenas and Luis and myself will hold a press conference. But by that time you'll have had the story out for almost a whole day. I made them promise me this. They owe it to me, after all. Oh, and there's also this."

Gato took an envelope from the inside pocket of his jacket.

"This is my personal statement about the reasons for my retirement. It's written in the form of a letter. A letter to you, personally. You could print it in that form. It might be quite unusual."

Faustino sat back in his chair and looked at the goalkeeper. His face was expressionless at first, but then a smile lifted into it like the rising sun. He stood up and went to the wall phone and took the receiver off the hook. Before he hit the buttons he turned back to the table.

"I have always wanted to say this," he said.

He punched the numbers, waited two seconds, and said, "Vittorio? Hold the front page."

Faustino made two long calls, during which El Gato sat patiently.

"Sorry about that, Gato," the journalist said when he finally sat down at the table again.

The keeper made a generous gesture. Faustino switched on the tape.

"Now," he said. "Why? You are thirty, which is not old for a keeper. You're at the top of the tree. You're playing better than ever, in my opinion. And you've won this." Faustino patted the bald dome of the World Cup. "So why retire now? You've got years left in you."

Gato said, "The reasons, the ones I want known, are in the letter. But you've answered your own question, Paul. Yes, I've got years left in me. I've got a life ahead of me, God willing, and I want to do something with it. Something more important than football."

Faustino recoiled in horror, raising his hands as if to protect himself from some evil apparition. "More important than football?" he cried. "I can't believe I heard you say that!"

He grabbed the microphone and spoke into it very slowly and deliberately.

"The world's top player, the great Gato, has just announced that there is something more important in life than football. In a moment, when he has stopped laughing, I, Paul Faustino, will challenge him to reveal what this thing is."

For some moments the tape machine recorded two men giggling like small boys in a school toilet.

Eventually Faustino said, "OK, my friend, what is it? You plan to take over the world, is that it?"

"Not exactly. Just save a part of it."

"And what does that mean?" asked Faustino, straightening his face.

"I owe a great deal to the forest," Gato replied, "and now I want to pay something back."

"Oh my God," Faustino said. "Are you telling me that you are giving up football to become a conservationist? One of those hippy Green campaigners?"

"Something like that," the keeper said. "And you are going to become one too."

"I am?"

"Of course. You're going to write that book with me."

"Hey," Faustino said, "wait a minute. If – and it's still if – I do this book, it'll be because the world is interested in you. And, to be frank, because it will make me money. And I'm no saint. I'm not going to give the money to some rainforest charity."

"No one's expecting you to. We'll go fifty-fifty on the book. What you do with your money is up to you. And what I do with my money is up to me."

The journalist leant back in his chair and drummed his fingers on the tabletop. He said nothing for a bit.

"So that's my headline in tomorrow's *Nación*, is it? El Gato Quits Football To Save Rainforest?"

The big man leant into the lamplight and fixed his eyes on Faustino's.

"No, absolutely not," he said, "because that will make

me sound like some sort of crank. I forbid it, Paul, really. Apart from anything else, it will spoil the surprise of the book when it comes out. You do see that, don't you?"

Faustino did see that, yes.

"And another thing," Gato said, "is that, as you say, I have won this." He put a large hand on the gold skull of the trophy. "What else is there? As far as football is concerned, I have done what I set out to do. Needed to do. Four years ago, when France knocked us out of the Cup in the semi-finals, I was devastated. The rest of the team were too, of course, but it was especially bitter for me. I felt like someone who had set out to climb Everest and been forced to give up just metres from the summit. Now I've got there. Four years later than I thought, but here I am."

He caressed the textured gold of the trophy. "It's not especially attractive, is it?"

Faustino switched the tape recorder off, stood up, stretched. "There's a couple of things I have to do. One more call to make. Turn things off. Then we'll go and get stuck into a serious breakfast. Is that OK? Five minutes?"

El Gato dragged his gaze away from the World Cup. "Sure," he said. "Whatever. Do you mind if I have a quick look around the Paul Faustino Library of Useless Knowledge?"

Faustino already had the phone in his hand. "Be my guest," he said. Then he started talking rapidly into the receiver.

He was still talking when Gato came out of the other room and said, "Paul?"

There was something, a vibration in his voice, that made Faustino look round straight away. The goalie had a book in his hands. Faustino recognized it. It wasn't a book exactly; it was a photo album. An old one, with padded covers of faded brown leather. Gato was holding it open, staring down at it.

"What, Gato?"

The keeper laid the book down on the table, in the lamplight, beside the World Cup. There was something so intent in the way the big man stared at it that Faustino said into the phone, "I'll call you back," and hung up. He went over to the table.

"What team is this?" Gato said.

Faustino looked at the photo, a small black and white picture fixed to the page with yellowing mounts. It showed eleven players in an old-fashioned group pose: five in front, crouching, six players behind, standing with their arms folded. A short man in a terrible suit stood at the end of the back row. The stocky man in the middle of the front row was obviously the captain. His hand was resting on a football. The shirts they wore had high collars and broad vertical stripes. Below the photograph, handwritten in fading ink, was a list of names arranged to match the players' positions in the picture.

"Don't you know?" Faustino said.

"Paul, I wouldn't have asked if I did," Gato said. There was impatience in his voice.

"Sorry," Faustino said. "I'm just surprised. But I suppose there aren't many photographs of these guys. This is the national side of 1948 to '50. The greatest side we ever had, or so they say. The Lost Ones."

"The Lost Ones? What do you mean?" El Gato didn't lift his eyes from the photo.

"They vanished," Faustino said. "By all accounts they were brilliant. Didn't lose a single game for two years. They were favourites to win the World Cup in Rio de Janeiro in 1950. These guys were better than Hungary or Italy. Way better, some say. They were going to bring the Cup here for the first time."

"What happened?"

"The team took off for Rio three days before the finals. But they never got there. Their plane went down in the jungle, presumably. It was pretty much all jungle between here and Rio in those days. They reckon they ran into one of those electrical storms. The army sent planes out for a week, searching. But they never found a thing. The jungle just swallowed them up. Terrible."

The phone rang. "Excuse me," Faustino said and went to answer it. Seconds later he heard the door close and looked round. Gato had gone. Faustino said "Wait" into the phone and went out into the corridor. It was empty, but the lift doors were shut and the red indicator light was moving down the floor numbers.

Faustino went back into his office. He should have gone back to the phone but didn't. He went to the table and moved the photo album further into the light of the lamp and studied it. He looked carefully at the photo of the Lost Ones. In particular, he looked at the tall figure in the middle of the back row. It was hard to get any real impression of what he looked like because he was wearing an old-fashioned cap, and the peak of it threw a dense shadow over the upper part of his face, entirely concealing his eyes.

Faustino was squinting at the names below the photo when he realized that the World Cup was no longer on the table.

THE HAWK RODE the rising air with the morning sun behind her. Her yellow eyes were fixed on the reddish-black track which cut through the trees far below her. This was the track along which the shiny fast animals ran. This was the track where the hawk fed now. She no longer had to trouble to hunt in the forest canopy, because the shiny fast animals killed but did not stop to eat. They left meat on the track where they had killed it, and then ran on, their low howling slowly dying away. The hawk did not understand this, nor care about it. All she had to do was wait on the wind for a kill and then stoop to take it.

She did not have to wait long. The track was still half shadowed by the low sun when the first stream of dust and the first glint of light reflected from the shell of a fast animal caught her eye. She readied herself, tilting slightly on the hot air.

The car was a slightly beaten-up Japanese four-wheel drive. Not the kind of vehicle to attract attention, which is why the man driving it had hired it, rather than the new Mercedes-Benz he had been offered. The road was rough in places, but much better than he remembered it. Traffic was light; logging in the forest ahead of him was just starting, and the heavy trucks carrying timber back down the road had not yet set out. Once or twice he swerved to avoid small animals. He reached the town at the time he had meant to – after the men had left, after the children had gone to school, and before the women had left their houses. He was surprised to see a sign on the road telling him where he was. It had not been there when he was last here. The town had no name to put on a sign back then.

The driver parked the Toyota beside the church and got out. After looking about him for a second or two – looking for watchers, perhaps – he opened the back door of the car and took from the seat two small bunches of white flowers and a small leather rucksack. He locked the car and then followed the rough pavement which led to the graveyard.

Although the graves were arranged in straight lines with equal spaces between them, no two graves were exactly alike. Some were gaudy, covered with tiny painted statues, plastic flowers, toys, little dishes filled with sweets, written messages, even football rosettes and cigarette-card portraits of players. Some were covered in clean white gravel, while others were bare rectangles of dusty earth outlined by rough stones. Most had plain white-painted headstones made of concrete, inset with little square hollows containing photographs behind glass. The photographs all showed people who looked as if death was the last thing on their minds.

Gato stopped in front of two graves side by side. Both were neatly bordered in pale pink stone and covered in white gravel. The headstones were unusual in that they were slabs of expensive marble. On one, the photograph was of a happy middle-aged man with a halo of wiry hair. On the other, the picture was of an old woman called Maria who had stared into the camera as if it had been a gun. Gato placed a bunch of his white flowers on each grave. Then, kneeling, he unzipped the rucksack and took out a medal attached to a loop of gold and purple ribbon. With his hand he dug a hollow in the white gravel of the man's grave, put the medal into it, and covered it over. After a few moments he stood up, lifted the bag and walked away.

He had expected some difficulty in finding the house, but it was easy. What surprised him, and worried him, was that it no longer stood at the edge of the forest. The town had hacked the trees back; the area behind the house where pigs had rootled and chickens had scuffed was now a rough street with cars parked in it. New houses sprouting TV aerials and satellite dishes occupied the space from which his paths had once wound into the forest. But the dark wall of trees was still there – pushed back, but still there; still close, still dark – and this gave him hope. He made his way round the back of the houses and, without much difficulty, found the track he was looking for. He followed it, feeling very uncertain because the last time he had tried to return he had failed and got lost. But this time the forest opened to him, led him in. He walked deeper into the trees, through the shattered darkness, as if he were following someone he could trust. So this time when he pushed aside the curtain of thick glossy leaves and walked into the impossible turfed clearing he was not in any way surprised. He walked into it like an ordinary man strolling onto his lawn on a summer's morning.

He walked through the dense silence to the goalmouth and put his hand against the left upright, feeling its ancient texture. Then he turned and went to the centre of the clearing, to the centre of the green space that had changed his life. He slid the leather rucksack off his shoulder and placed it on the grass. Then he stepped back a pace and waited.

The Keeper came out of the trees, a mixture of himself and his own shadow, as always. When he reached the edge of the trees' shade and moved into the light, his outline seemed to grow steadier. As before, his eyes were lost in the darkness below the peak of the old-fashioned cap. Five metres from El Gato he stopped.

El Gato had, of course, practised what he would say. Or, more accurately, he had practised many small speeches without choosing one. He did not know how much the Keeper already knew. He had hoped that the Keeper would speak first, but that didn't happen.

So, stupidly perhaps, El Gato said, "I have come back."

The muscles in the Keeper's face shifted awkwardly as if he were trying to dislodge something stuck in his mouth. As if he were remembering, slowly, how to speak. His lips moved, and the words came – slightly late, as ever.

"Of course."

Gato's words came out in a clumsy tumble. "I am sorry I took so long. It took much more time than I thought it would. I thought I would be able to come here four years ago. The thought of you waiting, of your long wait, has, has..."

"Has what, son?"

"Has troubled me. Haunted me."

The Keeper lifted a hand. "And it has made you great," he said. "It has made you complete something. And as for time..." He shrugged. "We are used to it. It is like rain to us – we knew it would stop, eventually. And that then we would be in the sun, at last."

"I was afraid," Gato said, "that you would think I had failed. That I would not come back."

"There was never any doubt," the Keeper said.

There was a silence then. The living man and the man who had not managed to die stood facing each other in the unnatural quietness.

The Keeper ended it. He said, in a controlled, formal way, "I believe you have brought something to us." He held out his arms as a father might reach for a child. Except that they were trembling.

El Gato opened the rucksack and took out something the size of a baby, something swaddled in a purple and gold shirt. He unwrapped the World Cup and carried it to the Keeper, and when the Keeper took it their fingers met briefly. It was the first time the men had touched. The Keeper's fingers were neither warm nor cold, but they left a faint print of numbness on the living man's hands.

The change that came over the Keeper was slight but also astonishing. Holding the Cup in his large hands, he became more solid. To Gato, it was as if a character in a movie had stepped out of the screen, or as if a reflection had materialized from a mirror. He was flesh, not air. He cast a shadow, a sharp defined shadow, on the grass. He lifted the trophy above his head and raised his face to it, and the light that flashed from the gold illuminated his features. For the first time El Gato saw the Keeper's eyes: intense black pupils within rings of amber. Glittering with tears.

The Keeper stood motionless for several moments.

And then the Lost Ones, the Waiting Dead, came out of the forest.

They appeared at first as a sort of interference in Gato's vision: darker shapes within the darkness of the trees. Then they moved out into the clearing, becoming men. They wore the old national shirts with their broad vertical bands of purple and gold. The captain, Di Meola, came first, then the plump little coach, Santino, in his ill-fitting suit. Behind him Miller, then El Louro, the fair-haired winger. Cabral, Vargas, Neruda, the others. They gathered around the Keeper, paying no attention to El Gato. Perhaps they could not see him. The Keeper lowered the World Cup and handed it to Di Meola. Di Meola kissed it and then crouched on the turf, placing the trophy in front of him. Two players crouched on either side of him and put their arms around each other's shoulders. The other six players, with the Keeper at the centre and Santino at the right of the line, stood behind with their arms folded. El Gato understood that he was looking, through his own tears now, at the living version of the photograph he had seen in Paul Faustino's office. Except that Di Meola's hand was not resting on a football, but on the trophy he had been destined to win. And these players were not living.

A sudden furious gust of wind, impossible on such a still morning, set the trees in motion. A quiet roar, like the rejoicing of a distant crowd, filled the clearing briefly. Gato looked up at the whirling treetops, delighting in their energy; and when he looked back at the Lost Ones they were already fading. The Keeper was the last to go, his right arm raised. His eyes died like stars in the morning light.

El Gato picked up the World Cup, a worthless, priceless

and magical chunk of metal. He wrapped it in the shirt, put it into the leather rucksack, and walked out of the clearing, into the trees. The curtain of thick glossy leaves closed behind him.

Almost immediately, the forest sent its thin green fingers out into the space he had left, feeling for new places to grow.

THE SECOND PAUL FAUSTINO NOVEL

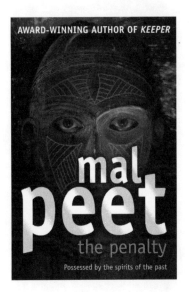

mal
peet
the penalty
Possessed by the spirits of the past

As the city of San Juan pulses to summer's sluggish beat, its teenage football prodigy El Brujito, the Little Magician, vanishes without trace.

Paul Faustino, South America's top sports journalist, is reluctantly drawn into the mystery. As a story of corruption and murder unfolds, he is forced to confront a bitter history of slavery, and the power of the occult.

WINNER OF THE CARNEGIE MEDAL

mal
peet
tamar

A story of secrecy and survival

When her grandfather dies, Tamar inherits a box containing a series of clues and coded messages.

Out of the past, another Tamar emerges, a man involved in the terrifying world of resistance fighters in Nazi-occupied Holland half a century earlier. His story is one of passionate love, jealousy and tragedy set against the daily fear and casual horror of the Second World War. Unravelling it will transform the younger Tamar's life.

"As fine a piece of storytelling as you are likely to read this year."
  The Guardian

"Beautifully crafted, with a finale that took my breath away, this is simply unforgettable."
  Publishing News

Branford Boase Award

Launched in 2000, the Branford Boase Award was inspired by the partnership of author Henrietta Branford and editor Wendy Boase, two very important figures in the children's book world, both of whom died in 1999. Designed to recognize the unique relationship between author and editor, the prize was greeted with great enthusiasm and after five years is now well respected and firmly established among the top children's literary awards.

The annual prize is awarded to an outstanding first novel for children, and the editor of the winning book also receives recognition for their contribution in identifying and nurturing new talent.

For more information, or to find out if a book you would like to nominate is eligible, see www.branfordboaseaward.org.uk

Winners of the Branford Boase Award have been:

2006   Frances Hardinge for *Fly By Night* (Macmillan
            Children's Books), edited by Ruth Alltimes
2005   Meg Rosoff for *How I Live Now* (Puffin Books),
            edited by Rebecca McNally
2004   Mal Peet for *Keeper* (Walker Books),
            edited by Paul Harrison
2003   Kevin Brooks for *Martyn Pig* (Chicken House),
            edited by Barry Cunningham
2002   Sally Prue for *Cold Tom* (Oxford University Press),
            edited by Liz Cross
2001   Marcus Sedgwick for *Floodland* (Orion),
            edited by Fiona Kennedy
2000   Katherine Roberts for *Song Quest* (Element),
            edited by Barry Cunningham